DRINK

HARMONY REED

STERLING & STONE

DRINK

Chapter One

I'M NOT TELLING you it's going to be easy, I'm telling you it's going to be worth it.

Nils remembered Jakob's words every morning, usually right as he was waking up. His sponsor first said them a year ago, almost exactly. Whether they worked as fuel for Nils's belief or as a salve when he needed it most, those eighteen words had already seen him through the worst of it.

He rolled over onto his stomach and reached for the coffee table, fumbling past his phone until four fingers found his eleven-month sobriety chip. They closed around it as he smiled.

Day 365. At tonight's meeting, he would trade the chip in his hand for one that promised the hardest year of his life was forever behind him.

I'm not telling you it's going to be easy, I'm telling you it's going to be worth it.

The first time Jakob said it, Nils hadn't believed him. He'd felt coerced into sobriety. Paloma made him feel he'd never have a chance with her again if he refused.

"You're not going to change by thinking you have more willpower than everyone else," she'd said. "A person can only get better once they finally decide they need to. And I can't make that choice for you."

Those last words left her in a whisper, which only made them more ominous. Then she'd fallen silent, but it was the sort of silence that fell between a detonation and the *BOOM*. Then she'd walked back into the house, leaving him to stand alone, stewing in his own stubborn bullshit.

He'd had no choice but to go.

Once there, he met Jakob. His new sponsor said the same things Paloma had, even if he used different words. But Jakob wasn't judgmental; he was familiar with Nils's particular breed of pain. He'd been through a version of the same thing himself. Jakob's pain made that promise easier to believe.

I'm not telling you it's going to be easy, I'm telling you it's going to be worth it.

Now, nearly a year later, his life would finally be returning to normal.

And what did *normal* mean, exactly?

A question that Nils couldn't stop asking himself. He used to include Paloma in his wondering, but that only seemed to piss her off. He wanted things to be the way they used to be, but she insisted that was impossible, no matter how hard he tried to show her that he changed.

Nils wanted *normal* back. He wanted family dinners and game nights, laughing without worrying if he was being too loud, and long walks holding Paloma's hand or playing hide-and-seek with Tyson. He wanted to sleep next to his wife, not on the foldout couch in the spare room.

After a quick stop in the bathroom, he headed to the kitchen for his first cup of coffee, catching the aroma of a just-brewed pot a few steps before he got there, which meant Paloma was in a better-than-usual mood. She wasn't in the kitchen, but Tyson sat at their small table, scooping oatmeal into his mouth. Two cheap plastic masks lay on either side of the birthday boy's bowl: Batman and Robin.

Nils made it halfway to the French press before Tyson ran to him, a mask in each hand. As usual, he waited to hear his father's footsteps before launching his morning attack.

Tyson thrust the Boy Wonder at Nils and said, "I'm Batman, and Mom is Batgirl, so you're Robin!"

Nils was about to take the mask when it occurred to him that this was a teachable moment, the kind of lesson his father was never around to help him learn. That celebrations were about generosity and sharing your joy with others. Not about being the center of attention and getting everything you want.

What was the point of sacrificing so much to get sober for Paloma and Tyson if the kid didn't benefit from his wisdom?

Pretending to be confused, Nils said, "But Batman is a grownup, and Robin is a kid, right?"

Tyson looked up at his father. Down at the masks, then up again.

"You should be Batman? Because you're the grownup?"

"It makes sense, doesn't it?"

Tyson hesitated, his heart obviously set on Batman, but he surrendered the precious mask anyway. "Are we gonna catch the Joker?"

Nils donned his plastic cowl and hooked his thumbs into the belt loops of his robe as if he were wearing a utility belt, staring off into the distance with a heroic expression. "We're going to catch ALL the bad guys!"

Tyson turned himself into the world's most famous sidekick and struck the same pose. "To the Batmobile!"

Ed — Nils had stopped calling him Dad in his head long before high school — never would've played pretend with his son before breakfast. Ed had spent most of Nils's childhood breakfasts sleeping off bender after bender at the VFW with his wartime buddies.

Ed hadn't even tried. Not like Nils was trying.

He couldn't have been prouder when Tyson karate-kicked an invisible supervillain who'd apparently been sneaking into the kitchen. "Great job, Robin. I've taught you well."

"Did Robin do a great job of finishing his breakfast?" Paloma. Dressed for work. Looking like *she'd* eaten a lemon for breakfast. She snatched the cowl from Nils's head and plunked it down on the counter. "If you're not going to help your son get ready for school, could you at least stop distracting him?"

Tyson scrambled back into his chair while taking the Robin mask off and dropping it beside his bowl. "I was just saying good morning to Dad."

"I understand that, but this is what happens every morning — you let your oatmeal get cold, then you refuse to eat it."

"I'll eat it, Mommy. I promise!"

Paloma yanked open the fridge and started pulling sandwich fixings out.

Nils tried not to show his annoyance. Sure, getting a healthy meal before school was important, but so were their father-son moments. The same moments Paloma had spent months yelling at him for missing just a year ago. How did she expect him to make up for lost time if he couldn't spend two minutes goofing around with his son before school?

You can't control Paloma, Jakob would say. *Focus on the things you can control.*

He could control whether he started a fight with her or let it go.

She was probably stressed about Tyson's party. She loved their son as much as he did; of course, she'd want everything to be perfect for his sixth birthday.

No doubt she'd forgotten that today was also a special day for the whole family.

Once Nils got his one-year chip, Paloma wouldn't be able to deny that he'd done what she asked him to: get sober, for her sake and Tyson's. Then everything would change. He just had to make it through today.

He went to the French press, filled the mug Paloma had already set beside it — the one with two crows sitting side by side above the caption, *Attempted Murder* — then joined Tyson, who was shoving oatmeal into his mouth as fast as he could, getting breakfast over with so he could have a few minutes with his dad. He really was a terrific kid, and Nils felt lucky to have him.

He'd be lucky to have Paloma too. She promised to reconsider their separation once he'd been sober for a year. He was going to do everything in his power to remind her how good they'd been together before his father's poisonous legacy ruined everything.

He would have his perfect family again, and life would go back to normal.

"I'm finished!" Tyson announced.

"Good job!" Nils said.

"Hurry up and get dressed. The bus won't wait on you, and I'm not taking you to school, even though—"

"I know, Mommy!" Tyson bounded up from his chair and ran out of the kitchen.

Nils looked over at Paloma, appreciating her for the

first time that morning, her long brown hair falling in tiny ringlets at her shoulders. A simple silver beaded bracelet slid down her graceful wrist as she tucked the freshly made sandwich into Tyson's lunchbox. That cornflower blue dress, fluttering just past her elbows and knees, one of his favorites — she'd been wearing that dress the night he decided to propose to her.

Coincidence? Or had she chosen it intentionally?

"You look hot in that dress."

Paloma gave him a dirty look, not appreciating his appreciation at all and ignoring his compliment. "Did you ask Tyson if he did his homework?"

"We'd barely said good morning when you came in here."

She turned around and emptied the French press into another mug. This one read, *After Monday and Tuesday, even the calendar says WTF.* "Right."

Nils walked over to the counter, but not so close she could complain he was crowding her.

"All I did was say good morning, and he handed me the masks. Of course, he's excited about his party tonight. What was I supposed to do, shove it back into his hand and ask him if he's finished his chemistry?"

"He's in first grade, Nils. You're supposed to be the responsible one."

"I don't know what I did wrong."

"I would really appreciate it if you would stop commenting on my appearance."

"You mean giving you a compliment?"

"That's not the kind of compliment I need this early in the morning."

"It's positive reinforcement, Paloma. I'm letting you know that you look great, prepared for the day, and ready to kick ass, like you always are."

"You didn't say any of those things. You said, 'you look hot in that dress.' Does that sound like the kind of compliment you should be giving me right now?"

"I waited until Tyson was out of the room."

"That's still not the point. Of all the things you could say to me, that's the best compliment you can think of?" Paloma shook her head, looking at Nils in the way that always felt like *here we go again.*

"I don't want to fight." He wished for his coffee or something to hold. His hands felt so naked and awkward. "I wasn't trying to insult you. You look great, prepared for the day, and ready to kick ass. Like you always do."

"I get the feeling that you don't understand what just happened."

Nils didn't know how to respond. He couldn't just admit what he was thinking, not without starting an argument.

Arguments were his kryptonite, and today Nils needed to be Superman.

"It's too early for compliments about the way you look. I get it, and I'm sorry." He looked at her, feeling hopeful.

Paloma didn't smile or tell him she appreciated how hard he was trying to make things right. "It's not just the time of day …"

"So, what? I can't compliment my wife at—"

"I thought you didn't want to fight."

"I don't," Nils said. "But I do want to understand what I did wrong, so I don't do it again."

"Are you still planning to handle the cake?"

"Yes, but can you please tell me what I can and can't say? I can't follow the rules if I don't know what they are."

"The Cooling Rack closes early today, and the cake won't be ready until noon, so you don't have much of a window—"

"Not communicating is how we got here." Nils did his best to channel Jakob's calm patience. "I'm ready to listen whenever you're ready to talk."

"Can you pick up the cake between noon and one, or not?" Now they were definitely back at *here we go again.* "If you can't, then I need to know now so I can plan my day accordingly. I'd rather not have Tyson's birthday ruined at the last minute, thanks to one of your usual surprises. Again."

That felt like a stab in the back, but … he had to admit it was fair. Tyson's birthday party last year had been his rock bottom. He'd failed both his wife and his son in the worst possible way.

It was time to prove that he'd changed.

"I've got it."

"*Promise?*"

Now he was pissed, but of course, he wasn't allowed to show that. Not unless he wanted to turn this conversation back into a fight that could destroy his plans for tonight.

He had to be the mature one. He'd done the hard work to break out of his negative patterns, but she refused to attend any meetings for the spouses of addicts, so she'd fallen behind. It was on Nils to lead by example and to be patient with Paloma while she caught up.

That was the hardest part of all this. He'd changed, but she couldn't see it because she hadn't.

"I promise to pick up Tyson's cake from the bakery between noon and one today."

"If you have a meeting or think you might need to blow this errand off for any reason, that's fine. Please just tell me so I can factor it into my day."

"Jesus, I'm not going to forget our son's birthday cake. Not after everything I've sacrificed to get sober for both of you."

She looked away and said, "Don't be late," before stalking out of the kitchen.

No acknowledgment whatsoever of his one-year anniversary.

He felt weak, needing her appreciation, but it ran like a current inside him. Not that Nils expected fireworks, but would it have cost her anything to congratulate him for hitting his milestone? The one that *she* had set for him?

Today meant everything, and tonight meant even more.

Chapter Two

SOME SURPRISING NEWS

THE DOOR CLOSED, and Nils felt like he could finally exhale.

The awkward bullshit would be over soon. Something to laugh about when they looked back and wondered how they ever doubted they belonged together. He just had to wait it out, ignore the frost and remind himself that their world would be warming soon.

No reason to lash out with the finish line right in front of him. He went to Paloma's bedroom, where he was allowed half a row in her miniature closet and the two bottom drawers in a dresser that once belonged to him, back when it was in a boy's bedroom with posters of Pearl Jam on the wall. Mom had turned it into a gym before her passing, so motivational posters graced the room instead. Slogans like *You can't spell LEGENDARY without Leg Day*, and *No matter how slow you go, you're still lapping everybody on the couch.*

He got dressed in jeans and a flannel, perhaps inspired by those thoughts of Pearl Jam. Or maybe it was the thought of what Paloma was going to say when she saw the delicate emerald pendant hiding in his gym bag. He'd skipped a matching set of rent payments to afford the stunning piece of jewelry, but the look in Paloma's eyes when he gave it to her tonight would justify the expense.

Not that Nils felt bad about skipping those payments. What kind of father charged his daughter-in-law and grandson rent to stay in his already vacant guest house?

The kind who was determined to humiliate his son for going to rehab.

Ed couldn't stand to see Nils's alcoholism reflecting back his own, so he made sure his son would feel worse about having to sell their old house to pay off the debt.

And Ed never had taken responsibility for passing his drinking problem on to Nils.

But enough of this. Jakob would tell him that he needed to let go of his anger — at Paloma, at his father, at the world — and focus on taking positive action.

Well, tonight, he was going to take the biggest positive action ever.

He was going to get his life back.

He only made it a few steps through the yard before the back door of the main house slid open.

Nils walked faster, pretending not to notice. Maybe he could make it out the side gate before Ed caught up to him.

But his father gave him an extra-friendly wave. "Nils, good morning!"

Maybe Nils had been wrong. Maybe Ed knew what day it was and wanted to acknowledge his son's year of sobriety.

"Morning," he said with a smile.

"Big day?"

"Yep." Nils nodded. "Big day."

Big day could have meant anything.

How hard was it to say, *Congratulations, son. Today is your one-year anniversary, right? Staying sober is a bitch, and so is being a great dad, so kudos to you for doing both.*

Ed decided to stick with being an asshole instead. "There's something I need to tell you."

"Of course there is."

"What's that supposed to mean?"

"Nothing, Dad. What is it?"

"Do you want to come inside?"

"I'd rather not." Nils glanced at the gate. "Big day, remember."

His father sighed, seemed to hesitate, then dropped the bombshell. "I'm selling the house."

"What?"

"It's too big for me and has been since your mother died. All of my money is wrapped up in this place. It's time to cash in for a better life."

"Why now?" Nils worked to keep his temper in check, surprised by how sudden and hot the rage felt inside him. "The market will only get better. Hang onto the place for another year or two and—"

"There's another buyer lined up al—"

"Another buyer? What the hell, Dad?"

"It's not like you need to leave overnight. You've got six weeks to—"

"Six weeks?"

"Yes, Nils." Ed's expression changed, disappointment like a bitter wind withering his face. "That's plenty of time. I'll help you find a place."

"I don't need help finding a place, Dad. That's not the issue. I don't want to uproot my family."

"Paloma and Tyson are already taken care of."

"What's that supposed to mean?" Something felt sick in his stomach.

There it was again, that pitying expression that made Nils want to grab his father by the shoulders and start shaking him. No matter what he tried, every conversation with Ed ended up here.

Because he loved to humiliate his son.

He couldn't pretend to have already known. But admitting that his own wife had rented a house and hadn't even told him? Or worse, finding out on the very day she'd agreed they would recommit to their marriage?

He could barely acknowledge that truth to himself. That Ed already knew — and had chosen to ambush him one last time while he was down — that was exactly the kind of shit he'd come to expect from his father.

Nils had to swallow his molten rage at Paloma, having kept him in the dark. His throat burned, and he was suddenly desperate for a drink. He licked his lips, hating that his father saw it.

"This is bullshit, Dad."

With his faux patient tone: "What exactly about it is bullshit?"

"You can't just sell the house I grew up in."

"Would you like to take over the mortgage payments?"

"You know I can't, and besides, there are only like two years left on the loan. You could refinance the place, and your payments would be like fifty bucks or something."

"So that's your advice? To hell with your father's retirement or any dreams he might have. Because you need access to your childhood home. Specifically, the guest house out back."

"That I pay rent for."

"I charge you a sweetheart rate, and apparently, even that isn't low enough to keep you honoring your end of the commitment."

"I'm a month late."

"It's two months, son."

"This month has barely even started!"

"Do you make that argument with your utilities? Your credit cards? Y—"

"I'm your son. You shouldn't even be charging me."

"You're my son, and too often, in times like this, I feel like I've failed you."

"You can make it up to me by not selling your house."

"Don't worry about what you owe or will owe. Consider it a gift."

As if that didn't make it ten times worse. *I'm destroying your life again, son. My gift to you.*

"The sale is final, as of today. I thought you'd want to know sooner rather than later."

"Just not sooner than Paloma."

"Paloma understands."

Nils didn't respond because he wanted to scream or hit something, not swallow his pride. It didn't matter to Ed Murray that he'd been an absentee father throughout Nils's entire childhood. It didn't matter that he'd had chance after chance to make it up to his son, now that Nils was an adult.

He'd spent the last twelve months playing Grandfather of the Year, and now he acted like that should absolve his decades of neglect.

"So where will you be, six weeks from now?" Nils asked.

"Florida."

"*Florida?*"

"Yes, Florida. This should only come as a surprise if you never listen. You know I hate the cold."

"California's not cold."

"I can trade California dollars for Florida dollars and

still get great year-round weather, beaches, and golf courses."

"When's the last time you went to the beach?"

"There's no income tax in Florida."

"You don't work anymore!"

"Exactly."

Nils wasn't the bad guy here, even if his father was making him feel that way. "You don't care about seeing Tyson grow up?"

"Of course I care. But Tyson is a part of my life, not my entire life. Same as you and Paloma."

Bullshit. Nils had never really been part of Ed's life. That was the problem.

"You literally couldn't have picked a place that's farther away and still have stayed in the states."

"Well then, it's a good thing I didn't go international. I'm sure I could live like a king in the Philippines."

"What's the harm in putting this off for a year?"

Ed gave him a patient smile. "Because, due to some unforeseen and rather lofty expenses, I've already been putting this off for a year."

He wasn't even being subtle with his accusations. Helping his son had forced Ed to delay his dream, and he wanted to make sure Nils got that.

"Fine, Dad. Congratulations. I'm super happy for you. It's great that you're moving to Florida and will barely ever see your grandson."

"Paloma's promised to bring him down whenever she can. And when he's older, Tyson can visit himself whenever he wants. It happens fast; he'll be driving before you know it."

Another bitter implication to swallow, that either Paloma or Tyson would be visiting without him. Ed had so little faith in Nils, he assumed that Paloma would divorce him.

Nils took a bit of grim satisfaction in the thought that at least he was going to be disappointed about that.

The situation would be so much more tolerable if his father wasn't pretending like he was some sort of parenting superhero. He'd never been there for Nils. Not for his baseball games, not for his basketball games, and not for any of his campouts. When Nils had been forced to abandon Boy Scouts due to lack of parental participation, did Ed apologize? No, he just said, *We can send you to Catholic school and let you hang out with the priests. It's basically the same thing.*

"You weren't there for me when I was growing up, and now you won't be there for Tyson. I don't know why I expected better from you."

Nils was hoping his father would take the bait. He needed a lightning rod for his anger, something to make him less thirsty for all the things he shouldn't drink.

Instead, Ed clapped Nils on the shoulder, and in his kindest voice, he said, "You have a second chance here, Nils. Please, be a better father than I was."

I already am.

Chapter Three

HUMAN RESOURCES

His phone buzzed again.

I know ur at work but if you have a minute I really need it.

Crissy, his sponsee. The morning had barely begun, but she was apparently in crisis already.

Nils peeked past the HR reception desk — no Stew in sight. The man was fifteen minutes late for his own reprimand. Not surprising, based on the written report Stew's supervisor had submitted yesterday, but still disappointing.

Crissy again: *I'm really close to having a margarita … give me a call if you're around.*

Where was Stew? Did he not understand that his job was at risk?

And how much longer did Nils need to wait before he could reasonably reschedule the meeting?

When he worked at the dealership — back when he was still in control of his drinking — his time was his own as long as he met his monthly quota. Here, it mattered that the boss see him at his desk, even when he wasn't in a meeting.

Then there was the paperwork.

Crissy: *knock knock, just thought I'd try again.*

It would be on him if she started drinking again. That was a sponsor's job. Even if Jakob wasn't there for him like he used to be, Nils wouldn't do the same thing to Crissy.

And it would be even more humiliating for Nils to fail a sponsee because it would mean Jakob had been right to drop him. When Crissy approached him the first time, the old man insisted Nils wasn't far enough along in his own journey to sponsor someone else.

Stew was nineteen minutes late. For all Nils knew, the problem employee was at a bar right now, tossing back a Jack-and-Coke and bitching about his job to the other day drunks.

It would be irresponsible for Nils to leave his sponsee waiting any longer on the off-chance Stew was going to show.

As he stood, a dark-haired man rapped three times on Nils's open door. "So sorry, traffic was terrible."

Nils gestured to the seat in front of his desk and texted Crissy back: *Sorry, I'm caught up with a couple of things right now. Go to Topped Off and wait for me. I'll get there as soon as I can.*

Crissy responded immediately: *OK.*

Then back to Nils: *Text me a pic of you drinking a cup of coffee so I know you're there and okay.*

OK, Crissy texted again.

Stew, now seated, drummed his fingers on his knees. Until a year ago, he'd been one of Ember Chemicals' model employees, but his performance had steadily deteriorated until Nils had no choice but to sit with him for an extremely uncomfortable one-on-one. He hated being the heavy; he'd rather inspire people than criticize them.

Hopefully, this would go fast, so he could take an early lunch and meet up with Crissy.

"Do you know why you're here?" Nils asked.

"I think so," Stew responded, looking embarrassed but holding his gaze.

"Do you want to tell me what's been going on?"

That question was apparently harder to answer. He looked down at the desk like an answer might be waiting in triplicate. Nils saw this often at meetings, a new member stuck somewhere between wanting to honestly answer the question and not wanting to condemn himself.

Stew finally shrugged. "I'm not sure."

Nils sighed, wishing Stew had tried harder to find a better answer — but at least there was no reason to draw this out. "Do you understand that Mr. Wilkes is done taking disciplinary action and has recommended that you be fired?"

Stew swallowed hard enough that Nils could both see and hear it.

But he still didn't answer.

Nils understood why, but Stew had to admit to having a problem if he wanted help. Same as everyone else who hit rock bottom. Otherwise, there was nothing he could do to protect the guy.

"I've been going through some stuff at home ..." Stew started before abandoning the sentence.

"Like ...?" prompted Nils.

"You know, the usual stuff. Arguments with my wife, my daughter's been getting into more and more trouble ever since she started middle school, my dog's even been shitting on the—"

"I don't mean to interrupt, Stew. But your dog making a mess is an even worse excuse for your poor performance than the family problems. Don't get me wrong, I'm sympathetic, and we do have options. But you're cuffing my hands by not being straight with me. This is your last chance to fix things before you get the pink slip. Please don't waste the opportunity."

Anguish twisted his face into a grimace. Nils had seen that same expression many times, including in the mirror, until he'd slain the dragons in his mind. Now he saw it at every meeting.

He put on his best Jakob face, the one that had gotten Nils through that first horrific month after rehab.

"It's okay. You're safe in this room." He gave that a moment to sink in, then settled back into his chair.

Stew finally sighed and leaned back too, like he'd just let go of the last shred of pride he'd been clinging to.

"Lisa left me …" He choked, coughed, then exhaled and reset himself. "It's the drinking. She said she's …" Another cough. "I've never seen her so furious."

Nils said nothing to see if more was coming. But Stew either needed a moment or some encouragement from Nils.

Three breaths, then, "Is she gone for now, or gone for good?"

There was a big difference, and while bottoming out, Nils had thought Paloma was gone for good. At first, he'd wanted to die.

"Gone, for now, I think." A thin glimmer of hope seemed to light Stew from within.

"How much are you drinking?" Nils asked, but he knew the answer was *too much*.

"She doesn't understand how much pressure I'm under, especially since Wilkes made base camp in my asshole." He flinched, already apologizing with his obvious shock. "I'm sorry, I shouldn't have said that."

Nils raised his hands with a reassuring smile. "It's fine. We're just talking here. So, why is Wilkes going places that only Lisa should be going?"

Stew smiled back, tentative but there. "He thinks I should be doing more than I am."

"Should you be?"

"It isn't that simple."

"Explain it to me."

"How candid can I be?"

Nils took out his phone, set a timer for ten minutes, then turned it around and showed the screen to Stew. "Anything you say until this timer goes off is a hundred percent off the record."

"Okay." Stew coughed. "I'm the only one on the team who knows how to run Gamma, so Wilkes is always barking at me to monitor the dashboard, but—"

"Mind if I interrupt?" Nils asked, though he already had.

Go on, said Stew's expression.

"Are you really 'the only one on the team who knows how to run Gamma'? Because I can't imagine that's true."

"I made the mistake of proving my competence with the platform. Now half the team pretends they don't understand the Gamma dashboard, even though it's pretty goddamned straightforward, and there are tutorials. The other half gets invited when Wilkes throws a barbecue."

"That's fair," Nils agreed.

"I'm already doing more than anyone on the team by managing the dash, but he also expects me to do other people's jobs, too. Check my file. I've worked more weekends than the rest of them put together." Stew leaned forward as if about to whisper. Instead, he spoke louder. "I started doing an extra thing, trying to be a team player, but now my kindness has turned into an expectation, and that's not fair."

"Have you talked to Wilkes about any of this?"

"I keep telling him that I can work *with someone* to build

simple procedures we can all follow, even though that's not my job either. Or if he can't bring himself to make his *friends* do their job, then we need to hire a second person to help. It can't all fall to me by default."

Stew shifted in his seat and drew a breath to reset himself. "By dinnertime, all I want to do is veg out. So I have a few beers to let off some steam."

"I meant it," Nils said. "About being honest with me."

"I am being honest with you."

"How many beers?"

"Maybe a six-pack." Then, after a pause where Nils didn't flinch, and Stew blinked twice, the man added, "Maybe two."

"When's the last time it was less than a six-pack?"

"A long time ago," Stew answered, more defensive than embarrassed now.

"And how do you think that's affecting your work?"

"Are we still off the record?"

Nils glanced at the timer and nodded.

"I know I fucked up, okay? But I have always tried, and I can try harder."

"Is the drinking making things better?" *Please answer honestly.*

"No." Stew shook his head, emphatic.

"Then why do you keep doing it?" Nils asked.

After a long time, Stew finally gave Nils the response he'd been waiting for. "Because I don't know how to stop."

Now he could help. Because now he knew Stew would accept it.

"Let's get a rep from Gamma to give us a live demo on the software. If everyone can ask questions, that should eliminate a lot of the excuses. And I'll see what I can do about getting someone dedicated to help you."

"Thanks, man." Stew looked surprised, almost astounded. "That's really helpful."

"I'm happy to do what I can, but you're going to have to do the hard part. You're not in control of your drinking."

The phone chimed — Stew's off-the-record time was up — then buzzed, flashing a pic of Crissy sitting in a corner booth at Topped Off, looking at a large cup of coffee like it had disappointed her.

It's decaf, so I'm not even sure why I bothered. Hurry! (and thx!)

"Your wife?" Stew asked.

"Sponsee." And he hated the idea that he was making her wait when she needed his support. But if he had a chance to save Stew as well ...

"I know what you're going through." Nils picked up a framed photo of Paloma and Tyson with their arms around him, posing in front of the school sign on Tyson's first day of kindergarten. He turned it around so Stew could see what Nils had almost thrown away. "I could have lost everything if I didn't wise up."

"Might be too late for me."

"No one drinks without reason. Once you know what that reason is, you can do more to stop it. That's the biggest thing that helped me: knowing *why* I was drinking in the first place. We all have our origin story. So you gotta ask yourself, *What's my radioactive spider?*"

Stew opened his mouth, but Nils didn't really want Stew to answer him. He wanted the guy to consider the wisdom behind the words.

"My father was responsible for the gamma rays that turned me into the Hulk," Nils continued. "Which is what I felt like whenever I started drinking. Especially as I got older. Started pushing to see how hard I could drink."

He'd told this story so many times, boiled it down to its

most powerful essence, turned it into the version that capti-
vated new members. The version that inspired Crissy to
beg him to sponsor her. It no longer bothered Nils to admit
how low he'd sunk.

Because as bad as he'd been, he still wasn't the story's
villain.

"Dad was never there, and he never gave a shit that I
was out partying with my friends. Mom was so alone, she
kept herself company with pills and alcohol, so I didn't
listen when she started screaming at me for doing the
same. I was a smart kid but a shit student. Teachers didn't
get me, and neither did the other kids. Unless I was drinking." He drew a breath before his next confession, a pause
in the perfect place to ensure that his next sentence landed.
"I thought about suicide a lot."

Stew nodded like maybe he'd been thinking about
suicide too. He was ready for Nils to throw him a rope.

Not yet.

"Then I met Ray in my sophomore year of college.
Philosophy major. His number one philosophy was *fuck
beer;* he was all about the hard stuff. He saw through the
veneer. How empty life was and how hard everyone was
pretending to be happy. I was so lost; everything he said
made so much sense. But then—"

"You got clean?" Stew interrupted. Like they often did.

"I got worse." Nils loved this part, teasing them with
hope before he showed them how low their lives could get.
"Ray dropped out. I barely graduated. But then I met
Loma. Started getting drunk on love instead of liquor."

"You quit for her."

"Learned to hide it, long enough to get her to marry
me. But we had a baby, and—" The pause was key to
getting that surge of sympathy. "—being a father
is *hard*, Stew."

24

"Lisa wanted kids. Wants kids. But I—"

"They're worth it." Nils was an expert at getting the story back on track when a newbie tried to derail it with their own uninspiring story. "Just like getting sober is worth it."

Stew nodded, didn't interrupt as Nils told the rest of it: drinking binges with Ray that turned into weekend benders, mistakes at work that Paloma tried to help him cover up, the nights where they screamed at each other while Tyson cried quietly in the next room.

"Then I hit rock bottom at my own son's birthday party. The worst thing is, I was blackout drunk. My wife told me the next day—"

He let his voice catch. Not hard, since he could never take back the things he'd done and desperately wanted to.

"—after she kicked me out of the house I bought for her."

Stew swallowed another one of those annoyingly loud, moist noises that probably drove his wife crazy even before he'd started drinking. Nils ignored it and moved in for the closer.

"Even losing Paloma wasn't enough to wake me up. But when she said she'd never let me see my son again—"

"She can't do that. Can she?"

"I believed that she would, and that's what mattered."

"What did you do?"

"Checked myself into rehab. Haven't had a drink since. And now we're back together again."

Or at least they would be, after tonight.

"Wow, that's amazing. How long ago was that?"

Nils drew the chip from his pocket like the trophy it was and displayed it between his thumb and pointer for Stew. "This is my eleven-month chip. I'll get my one-year tonight."

"Really? No shit! Congratulations, man. That's great."

It was great. Sure, he'd left out a few details. How his father had basically forced him into rehab. How Jakob had to babysit him for the first month to keep him from falling off the wagon. How Paloma had given him her ultimatum about staying sober for a year if he wanted her back.

But too many details spoiled the story. Stew didn't need to know everything, he just needed to know enough to be inspired to start his own journey.

Nils flashed an encouraging smile and said the same thing Jakob told him at his first meeting.

"Last thing I want is to see you making the same mistakes I did. I can help you if you let me."

"I really appreciate that." Stew looked like he might cry. "Just tell me what to do."

"One second." Nils held up a finger, then grabbed his phone and sent Crissy a text.

Leaving the office in five.

His phone buzzed with her reply: *you do know this place is right next to a liquor store, right?*

He texted, *be there soon,* then slipped the phone back into his pocket and returned his attention to Stew. "The company has a program that pays for eight weeks of rehab at an approved facility. Your job will be held for you until you return."

"I thought you were going to f—"

"Once you're back, Ember Chemical will pay for weekly therapy for six months. After that, your insurance will kick in."

"The company would do that for me?"

"It gets even better." Nils loved this part. It was only the second time he'd had a chance to rescue someone like this. "Wilkes won't be able to fire you until after you're finished with the six-month probationary period. It's there to give you a chance to prove yourself. Once you formally ask for help, that can only be taken away from you in a case of grievous misconduct."

"I don't know what to say."

"Just promise me that we'll never be sitting across from each other having this conversation again."

"I promise." Stew stood and extended his hand.

Nils shook it, already thinking of Crissy.

Who was probably counting the change in her purse right now to see if she had enough for a bottle of cheap vodka.

He couldn't let her throw away all the progress they'd made because of Stew.

He walked Stew to the door, then closed it behind him.

But he didn't get far.

Angie, the department admin, called out from the reception area. "Your nine o'clock is here, Mr. Murray. Shall I send him in?"

Chapter Four

A RUSHED INTERVIEW

Nils was flustered.

No, *fuckered* felt more like it.

Nils usually prepared for interviews by going over the applicant's resume and LiveLyfe feed to help him establish a good rapport so he could sniff out the exaggerations and come up with his own estimation of strengths and weaknesses. But last night, he'd forgotten to do the usual prep. He'd been so wrapped up in the plan to get his family back.

"Of course," he called back. "Send him in."

Nils went back into his office and opened his calendar to check the entry for the link to the relevant application package — but it wasn't there.

At least he wasn't the only person falling down on the job today.

The door opened, and a fresh-faced college kid poked his head through the opening. "May I?"

"Of course," Nils said, trying not to sound irritated. Of course, he could come in; hadn't Angie just told him that? He gestured to the chair where Stew had been sitting just a minute before.

The kid sat.

And Nils realized he didn't know the kid's name. Or what position he'd applied for.

Fine, he'd wing it.

"Tell me why you want this job."

"Now that I've gotten my chemical engineering degree — did I remember to put on my resume that I graduated with honors?"

Nils managed not to roll his eyes. "Very impressive."

"I saw your ad on WorkIT and love what it implied because it really does seem as though Ember puts the future first. But what does that mean?"

Nils had no idea. "What do you think it means?"

"We all know that the chemical sector has been strong for a long time, outperforming the total market and most of its raw material suppliers. All thanks to the industry's ability to increase earnings on a base of total revenues and invested capital that's maturing slower, at a rate tracking close to global GBD growth."

Goddammit, this kid was giving him a headache. And he needed to text Crissy. Let her know that he'd been shanghaied into an interview.

How long would she wait before she gave in to the craving for a margarita?

She would try to resist, but without Nils's guidance, she'd have dropped out of the program after a week.

"But it seems like that golden era is coming to an end." The kid looked like he was enjoying giving this lecture. Nils wondered what industry magazine he'd cribbed it from. "We look at the indicators and see that while the last decade appears to have been good, the industry's return on invested capital has flattened, and for some subsectors has actually decreased."

"Your point?"

"I guess I'm just curious if everything works out and we start working together, how much mobility will I have within the company? Can I choose a position where I know I'll be able to make a bigger contribution?"

Why didn't he just ask that in the first place? Had Nils been that much of an ass at that age?

"I'll go anywhere the company needs me if I'm lucky enough to land the gig. I'm just trying to say that I've studied the market a lot, so for me, it's not just about the job; it's about where the industry itself is headed."

"I understand." Enough playing defense. Time to wrap this up. "What are your biggest weaknesses?"

Most applicants flubbed this one, especially if the question came this early on with so little rapport established. They'd hit him with some bullshit they'd memorized, using the question as an opportunity to aggrandize themselves by transforming some minor flaw into a strength: *My biggest weakness is getting so absorbed in delivering quality work that I lose all track of time.*

But the kid surprised him. This time by not answering immediately. It looked like he was actually thinking, which gave Nils the moment he'd been wanting.

He snatched up his phone. *Almost done, keep nursing that coffee.*

No reply. Was Crissy already gulping down a tart margarita, licking a crystal of salt from her lips as the heady burn of tequila warmed her throat?

Fuck. Now he wanted a margarita.

No, you don't. You just want to get out of here and make sure Crissy's okay.

The kid finally said, "I guess I'm working hardest at

owning when I mess up. I feel like I can always eventually listen to reason, but it takes longer than it should for me to admit my mistakes. But I am giving that attention and think I'm improving."

Decent answer. But it didn't make him like the kid more. Not when Crissy could be about to fall into a bottle, proving that Jakob had been right: Nils wasn't ready to sponsor someone else.

Nils forced a smile, then tossed a longing glance at his phone. The screen didn't light up with a reassuring reply.

"How about your biggest strengths?"

"It took me a long time before I finally realized it was a strength, but I'm great at saying the thing that no one else will."

The kid delivered that line with total confidence. Nils remembered his own job interviews, stuttering and nervous through every one of them, sick to his stomach and feeling like he had to shit the entire time.

It wasn't easy when you grew up without support.

The kid probably had an awesome father, who gave him everything, told his son he could do whatever he wanted in this world and went out of his way to make sure he felt loved.

It must be nice.

Nils forced himself to ask, "For example?"

"I was interning at SilverStar when a bunch of us, all in our twenties, were called into a room for some sort of focus group. They didn't tell us what it was, but there were several marketing execs in there, and I could tell right away that they wanted our opinions because of our ages. Turns out, that was exactly it — they were trying to rework their reputation by focusing on millennials. Everyone in the room kept trying to put makeup on the monster, but I suggested something more incendiary."

From the smug look on the kid's face, Nils was pretty sure that what came next was supposed to impress him. "Go on …"

"I suggested that SilverStar go with: *Yes, our company has made mistakes, and we've learned from them.*"

Nils kept his face neutral, mostly to let some air leak from the kid's ego. "Did they take your suggestion?"

"They let me go a week later." Said proudly. He clearly saw himself as someone who was taking on the establishment, without any awareness that if he got the job, he'd be working *for* the establishment.

Like Nils, before he'd fallen for Paloma and realized that a little respect went a long way toward getting his ideas taken seriously by her father.

Was he really feeling bad for this kid?

His phone buzzed. Crissy needed him.

He shoved sympathy — or was it pity? — aside and stood, smiling again. "Thank you for your time, we'll be in touch."

The kid looked up at him, mouth dropping open. "But—"

"We'll be calling candidates in for the second round next week." And he would make sure to give the kid another chance then, so he couldn't complain that Nils hadn't taken him seriously. Today was too important. He couldn't afford to fritter his minutes on anything less than returning his life to normal.

"But you barely asked me anything."

"I respect your time too much to waste it with irrelevant questions." Nils nodded toward the door as he scooped his phone up and slipped it into his pocket. "Here at Ember, that's considered a strength."

"But what about my experience? My transcript? Don't you want to see my references?"

"I want to see if you respect my time."

Nils left his office — the kid could figure out how to make a graceful exit for himself.

Right now, Crissy needed him, and Nils needed to help her.

Chapter Five

TOPPED OFF

A BARISTA CALLED out as he entered the coffee shop: "Nils? White chocolate mocha?"

His favorite.

It was like the world had been messing with him all morning and just decided that enough was enough, time to give Nils a pat on the back and congratulate him on his special day.

Then the surreal moment passed, and he realized that Crissy must've ordered it for him.

She waved to him from a table near the back of the café.

He picked up his mocha and raised it in salute while crossing the room. He sat across from her, then took a sip and smiled. The coffee at Topped Off was always strong, but the current of sweet from the white chocolate syrup cut the bitterness on his tongue.

"How did you know?" he asked.

"The last time we got coffee, you said that your wife doesn't like it when you order 'dessert drinks.' But those of us trying to stay sober know how much the sugar actually helps. Besides, today is a special day, right?"

Crissy's understanding filled up that empty space inside him with something warm and gooey and sweet like honey. Yes, it was a very special day indeed. And she was the first person in his life to give a damn.

But how did she know white chocolate mochas were his secret addiction?

Maybe he'd ordered one before, and she'd remembered.

Maybe she'd asked, and the barista had remembered.

Was that crossing a line? Or was she just trying to be nice? Jakob had warned him that having good intentions didn't keep you from making mistakes. And it would be very easy to make a mistake with Crissy.

A mistake that wouldn't just jeopardize his status as her sponsor — it would jeopardize his future with Paloma and Tyson, too.

"Your timing is amazing. How'd you know when to order it?"

"We have a special connection." Then, maybe responding to the uncertain look that usually found his face after Crissy said something at least slightly inappropriate, she added, "That's why you're my sponsor."

Okay, time to refocus Crissy on his reason for being here. "What's up?"

"Guess who showed up on my doorstep this morning?"

He didn't need to. Ruben, Crissy's crazy ex-boyfriend, who she apparently couldn't help herself around, had been the focus of all their conversations for the last month. It sounded to Nils like they didn't really have a relationship so much as marathon fuck sessions that left her damaged, dehydrated, and desperate for a drink.

"It must've been Santa Claus, apologizing for being so late with last year's gift. No, wait, was it Ed McMahon, delivering your sweepstakes m—"

"Who's Ed McMahon?"

"Never mind," Nils said. "So what did Ruben want? The usual?"

"Pretty much." Crissy took a sip of her coffee and made a face. "I've been sipping this so long it's gone cold."

"I'll buy you a new one after we've talked." An implied rebuke for the veiled complaint about how long it had taken him to answer her call. "Last time, you said that you weren't going to answer Ruben's texts. And that if he came over, you wouldn't open the door."

"I know, I suck. But I can't stop myself when it comes to him."

"How hard are you trying?"

"Harder than you think." Then she laughed and added, "And he's harder than you think, too."

"I'm not sure you should be making a joke out of it."

"I'm not, really. That's actually part of the problem. It's not that I'm in love with Ruben anymore, believe me, I'm not, but he fucks me like Johnny Deep. His dick is big but not too big, and even though he's a selfish fucker — *literally* — I always come, no matter what."

"Who's Johnny Deep?" Then, "You can still say no, Crissy."

"In theory, sure." She took another sip. "But he didn't text, he just knocked on my door. The moment I opened it, he was unbuttoning his pants, so like a second later, I was getting down on my—"

"That's enough."

"I'm just trying to give you context."

"You've told me multiple versions of this story already." Nils smiled to let Crissy know he wasn't rejecting her. "So.

I'll ask the same question as last time: *Why do you keep doing this to yourself?*"

She shrugged, took another sip, then leaned back in her seat. "You know how it is, Nils. It's hard to tackle more than one vice at a time. I'm giving up alcohol, do I have to give up sex, too?"

"I'm not sure that giving up sex is the problem here."

"What's that supposed to mean?"

"There's obviously some dynamic between you and Ruben that's feeding the compulsion. You could take care of your needs with Tinder or fkt or any of the other hookup apps out there."

"That's different." Crissy shook her head. "I'm not looking for anonymous sex."

"I thought you said you used to love anonymous sex." It made Nils uncomfortable to remind her, especially since it was slightly arousing, but he had to do his job as her sponsor. Keep her honest.

"I do, but it isn't helping. That's just feeding a different addiction."

"But things with Ruben clearly aren't good, right? What happened after … the two of you were finished?"

"After the first round, we did it three more times." Crissy giggled. "It was great."

"Until he left."

The mirth disappeared from her face. "Right, until he left."

"What happened then?"

"He left the bedroom to make himself a sandwich, but then he never came back. He was just gone without ever saying goodbye."

"So, exactly like last time. Why do you think he does that?" Crissy looked away, but Nils could still see the hurt. Now he felt like an asshole. It was his job to keep her honest, not to rub her nose in her mistakes. "I'm sorry—"

"No," she shook her head again, "it's fine, really. I knew what I was doing and hated myself the whole time, but it's still better than drinking, right? That's why I called you. The only thing keeping me from heading straight to the bar after I realized he was gone was knowing you'd be here for me."

Crissy's smile was slightly bent and in just the wrong way. Nils found himself thinking it looked sexy, as inappropriate as that thought so obviously was.

"I know I keep doing the same thing over and over and expecting different results, and I know that's the definition of insanity, but I just can't seem to stop myself or …"

Nils watched her face, waiting for Crissy to continue.

But she couldn't go on, and after a long and excruciating moment, her expression finally cracked. "Why does this always happen to me?"

It was the right question, but Nils didn't know how to answer. Or how to get Crissy to.

Ruben wasn't the real problem, he was only a symptom. The guy was an emotional vampire, but Crissy always opened the door for him. There were others too: she'd told Nils several stories in the short time he'd known her, about guys she'd met through dating apps.

The one who'd told her she was a slut afterward, adding that she should "maybe hit the gym to tighten that shit up."

The one who'd secretly filmed her then sent her a link to the site where he posted his trophies.

The one who'd left bruises from her neck to her knees, but sent her a rose for every mark the next day.

She'd even had a stalker from church who was obsessed with her. She'd tried going because AA encouraged it, and she was trying to "play full out." But after Melvin — "he even *sounds* like a stalker" — kept appearing like a specter wherever she went, she'd given up on church and gotten a restraining order.

Ruben was the lesser of many evils, a stopgap to help Crissy avoid dealing with the deeper issue.

Nils took her hand and squeezed it. "Your dad used to slap you around when he was drunk, right?"

Crissy nodded. "After he finished with my mom."

"We've talked about this before. You have legitimate reasons for your patterns, and this is not about blame. But it is on you to break out of your family's destructive cycles. My dad isn't anywhere near the dickhead that yours apparently is, but I've still fought hard to figure all of this shit out. You can do this, Crissy. You're doing it already. You just need to stay strong."

"Thanks for saying that." She looked at Nils in adoration, allowing her gratitude to sit between them like a silent invitation. "You always know the right thing to say. You make me feel seen. And heard."

She squeezed his hand, and suddenly he wasn't sure it had been the right thing to say at all.

Jakob was right: walking the line that separated supportive from inappropriate was tougher than he'd thought it would be.

Crissy was pretty, and she looked up to him. It was natural for that to stir something inside him. But he'd been aware of the potential to take advantage of her emotional vulnerability and had always treated her like he'd treat his daughter if he had one. She was almost young enough that she could be, and he was still married.

Yes, it stroked his ego that she was interested. That she listened to his advice and took it. That she didn't see him as the failure that Paloma did.

But he would never let it go any further than this.

He pulled his hand back and sipped his coffee, and so did she, a cumbersome silence resting between them. But Nils couldn't answer her the way she probably wanted him to, so he would have to wait her out.

"So, anyway," she finally said, "before you got all embarrassed and stopped talking to me, you were saying that a lot of this is my dad's fault, and I do agree, that man was a monster. But I could still do better than I'm doing right now, you know what I mean?"

Nils looked her in the eyes and nodded.

Seen and heard.

"Have I ever told you about Ross?" Crissy asked. "The one who made me wear a leash?"

Nils shook his head. "We've talked about the—"

"I shouldn't have said *made me*. That implies I did it against my will. He asked me once, and I said, *of course.* It was actually fun for a while. I'd just do whatever he told me to, you know?"

If she wasn't going to take the hint, it was up to him to steer their conversation to where it needed to go. Toward Crissy's need to confront her childhood abuse.

"That isn't a shared experience for me," Nils said, putting on his best tough-love face, "but the root emotion is universal. You just want to feel loved."

"And get face-fucked, if that's how he likes it." Crissy laughed.

"Do you think you might have a sex addiction?"

"Oh, *totally,*" she said, as though this was excellent news. "But I don't think that's a *problem, not* like drinking. Sex is natural. I mean, I get it, you're a little older than me," Crissy laughed, "but you've said it plenty. We're the fkt generation. If I want dick, I can get it an hour from now."

"Addiction is addiction. It doesn't matter what form it takes." Then he added something he'd said to her plenty of times before, enough to make it part of her permanent vocabulary. "The definition of insanity is doing the same thing over and over again, but expecting different results."

As if she hadn't heard him, Crissy continued, "It isn't having a lot of sex that's the problem. It's having it with all those different people. All the drama that comes with it. Like with Ross."

"You mean because of the leash?"

"I told you, I was fine with the leash. But then he started getting *really fucking possessive.* He hit me once." She appeared to think. "Twice. The third time didn't count because I hit him first. Point is, he turned into an asshole."

"Maybe you accidentally gave him the idea that you didn't mind being led around."

"Fuck you," she laughed. "You're supposed to be on my side."

"I am on your side."

"The last guy who was on my side got his cum all over it." Another laugh, almost a chortle.

"I'm not sure that's appropriate." It wasn't, and the twitch in his dick confirmed it. How was he going to get this conversation back on track?

"You want to help me, right?" She licked her lips like she was suddenly thirsty, despite having just finished a huge mug of coffee. "You can't do that if you don't know what the problem is."

"There is such a thing as too much information. It's enough to say, 'I've made mistakes by looking for love in all the wrong places.' I don't need to know about the leash, or the butt plugs, or anything else."

"I never said anything about butt plugs." Did she have to say that so loud? Half the café was looking in their direction. "And I'm not 'looking for love in all the wrong places.' Partly because I'm not a stupid country song from before my time—"

"It's before my time, too." Though Nils didn't know that for a fact. Still, her suddenly casting him as old felt like a bee sting.

"—and partly because love has nothing to do with wanting to feel a dick moving around inside me."

"Can you please … just … not." The problem in his pants was expanding.

"Not what? How many times have you told me that we can talk about anything?"

"This is different."

"Why?"

"Because you're being explicit. I don't need to hear about anyone's dick inside you," Nils said, especially since picturing it was making his do a little dance. What was he thinking, letting the conversation swerve into such dangerous territory?

"What I'm trying to say is, I'm not looking for love, but I do love sex. I'm *always* thinking about it. Drinking helped me to turn that part of myself off, or at least lower the volume. When I'm sober, I'm climbing the walls. When I'm fucking, I forget that I'm sober. Understand?"

"I understand," Nils said, trying to sound neutral.

He could relate. Right now, all he wanted was to get drunk and fucked. Preferably both.

How had he ended up here? He was supposed to keep Crissy from derailing her sobriety, but instead, she was derailing his.

"I don't need to stop having sex. If anything, I need to be having *more* of it. With a sane, stable man whose sex drive matches mine." Crissy reached across the table for his hand before he realized what she was doing.

Reality crashed in around him. Jakob had been right. He never should've agreed to be Crissy's sponsor.

Temptation called up a drunken memory from his college days: two girls in a dark bar, Ray claiming dibs on the brunette, the blonde laughing as she spilled a tall margarita all over herself.

She'd told him he could do anything he wanted to her, then with a whisper, she repeated, *anything at all.* But all Nils wanted to do was lick it off her. It haunted him now, the remembered tang of tequila and citrus and her.

He'd bet Paloma's emerald pendant — an awful thought in itself — that Crissy would let Nils do whatever he wanted to her, including drenching her in a margarita then licking her dry.

And right now, that was exactly what he wanted to do.

"I've always been attracted to older men." She squeezed his hand again as she practically batted her eyes. "It's a special day for you, right? Don't you want to celebrate?"

The pain of a wedding ring digging into his flesh pulled Nils from a trance of need he should never have fallen into. He'd gone through hell to get sober and wasn't going through it again. Not for her.

And not for anyone.

He yanked his hand back. "I'm your sponsor, not your boyfriend."

"I know that—"

"It's time for you to find someone else to help you—a woman. You need a sponsor with better insight into what it's like to deal with your dating life. Because, yes, you should be able to talk about that. But not with me. It just isn't appropriate."

Crissy blinked several times, fighting off the tears. She

was successful at keeping them away, but not without looking like Nils had destroyed her.

"I'm so, so sorry … you're absolutely right, and I didn't mean to make a mess of things. It's just that you've been so wonderful to me, and you're the only reason I've managed to stay sober so far. This is my third try, and I've never made it this long. I didn't mean to make you uncomfortable, and I promise that if you stay my sponsor, I'll never ever do anything like that ever again."

"It's not—"

"I'll do whatever you say. I mean, I'll follow whatever guidelines you lay down. I just don't want to slip back into my old habits. Please, Nils." Another laugh, just sweet and soft enough to finally break him. "Don't abandon me because I made a mistake."

"I'm married. You can never forget that."

"Hope to die." Crissy crossed her heart. "Can I get you a coffee to go, please? For being such an asshole?"

Nils accepted, then left Topped Off a few minutes later, sipping his coffee but thinking about margaritas.

He'd walked away from Jakob to sponsor Crissy.

How many other mistakes had he made since leaving rehab?

Chapter Six

A BRILLIANT IDEA

NILS WONDERED if Madison Lewis could tell he was gritting his teeth.

He was doing his best not to show it. Still, the silent agony of maintaining his patience was surely straining his face.

It was definitely taxing his ability to think about something else besides margaritas.

"Sorry." Ember's newest employee looked up from her paperwork. "My father always told me that I should never sign anything without reading every word, no matter how long it might take."

Maybe she'd like to hear a list of things Nils's old man had told him. Probably not, especially if he screamed them at her like he wanted to yell:

Would you please just sign the fucking thing?

It was a job offer. Whose terms he already verbally explained to her. All she had to do was initial each page to verify that she understood what he'd said.

What could she possibly expect to find that would be

worth turning down the job she'd been negotiating with him for the past week?

"Is there something specific you're looking for? Maybe I can help you find it."

She looked up and smiled at Nils. "I promise, I'm almost done!"

"Take your time," Nils said.

But they had been at this for forty-five minutes now, and he had been thinking about margaritas for most of that time, despite his desire to think about literally anything else. Except Crissy, or all the things she would probably agree to let him do to her, whether he bought her a margarita or not.

Madison had ambushed him the second he got back from Topped Off, after having waited for fifteen minutes herself. Angie should've had her fill out all of the forms while she waited, so he could give Madison the orientation speech and send her on her way. Instead, she left Nils to fumble for the second time that day, figuring everything out on the fly because Angie not only forgot, she'd also decided to take a break as soon as she passed Madison off to him.

What was the point of having an admin if she left the administrative work to him?

"Almost done!" Madison announced, which just made the fact that she wasn't done even more infuriating.

By the time Ember's newest employee finally deigned to sign her employment contract, Angie was back at her desk, a medical mask covering the lower half of her face. Because, of course, this day was going to keep getting worse.

Nils used up the last of his patience ushering her out. He barely managed to wait until Madison had turned the hallway corner before he said to Angie, "Are you kidding me?"

"What?" Angie looked like she didn't have a clue what he was talking about, even touched her lower neck in what had to be mock confusion. Then, to punctuate the absurdity, she coughed.

"That's what," Nils said, looking from Angie to the bottle of cough syrup on her desk, sticky purple bullshit bleeding out of the lip to drool on the bottle. "You work in HR. You should know the policies better than anyone."

"I got tested on my way in to work. That's why I was late. It's just a cold."

"So you thought it would be a great idea to share that cold with the rest of us."

"I'm wearing the mask. I've had the latest vaccine. I'm staying two arm-lengths away from other employees." She coughed again. "I'm following policy. Look it up."

"How about I look at your job duties? Last time I checked, you were supposed to have new hires read and sign their contracts before handing them off to me."

"I told her to complete them all before knocking on your door."

"Well, she didn't."

Nils looked at her for a moment so she could feel the full weight of his disappointment. "If you're not going to actually do your job, there's no point in you coming to work."

Angie shrugged. "I used up all my sick days last month."

He stomped back into this office, closed the door behind him, and sat at his desk. Email. Some mind-numbing cc's and memos were just what Nils needed before returning to neutral.

But as he started scrolling through his inbox, his mood turned to vinegar.

An urgent notice about that batch of workers' comp

forms he was supposed to have processed weeks ago. He would've loved to blame Angie, but he was the one who'd let the case files stack up, telling himself that it was easier to do them all at once, so he might as well give everyone involved in the accident a chance to submit their claims.

And then he told himself that there were so many to process, he'd need an entire afternoon without meetings to get through them all.

If the people here didn't drive him insane, the paperwork eventually would.

He forced himself to download the claims documents. If he started now, he might be able to get them all finished before it was time to leave for Tyson's party.

But that thought only worsened his mood. Made him think even more about those margaritas. And the bare skin he wished he could be licking them off of. He resented Crissy for putting both into his head.

He wondered if he'd ever made Jakob want to break his own sobriety streak.

Nils sighed, missing the days when he worked for Paloma's father at the Ford dealership. Before they were lovers, he and Loma were an unofficial team. She was the financing officer. Nils would hook a customer into buying a car, then hand them off to her for the paperwork. He countersigned the sales agreement and complimented their judgment in selecting the lot's very best car.

Back in the good old days, before a lifetime of emotional abuse from Ed had driven him to start over-drinking.

Nils should have started on the workers' comp claims, but instead, he kept scrolling, searching for a fragment of good news to lighten his mood.

Another twenty-four emails down, his heart missed a beat. Something from the Internal Revenue Service. Nils doubted they were sending him an email to congratulate him on a year of successful sobriety.

He opened the email, and his eyes immediately fell on the word *audit*. Shit. But not for this year's return, for last year's. Thanks to an apparent discrepancy between his reported income and what had been reported by his employer.

Goddamn fucking shit.

Another "gift" from his father. Because that had been the year that Nils had agreed to help out at Ed's plumbing company, doing odd jobs like ordering parts and calling customers to collect on unpaid invoices. It had been pure charity — after being fired by his father-in-law, Nils had lost a series of increasingly shitty jobs as his drinking increased. He'd assumed that Ed was paying him under the table, but apparently, his charity only went so far.

It figured that fucker would treat Nils like he was just any other employee and report his income to the IRS. Regardless of the consequences.

Nils ignored how hard his heart was pounding as he dialed. His call went directly to a phone tree with a bewildering array of options. He pressed zero enough times that his call was finally rerouted to the human he'd been waiting for the entire time. It wasn't like he could charm a recording into canceling the audit.

Nils told her why he was calling, gave his case number, and calmly explained that it was all a misunderstanding.

"I'd be happy to help you with that." Julie asked for his name and all the relevant information required to pull up his file. All information that Nils had already entered several times at various points along the phone tree.

"So, how is your day going?" Nils asked while she was looking things up.

"Fine." Then silence, not even the sound of her typing.

A few moments later, he tried again. The better a "customer" he was, the better his customer service would probably be. "How's the weather where you are?"

"My office doesn't have windows."

Nils didn't bother Julie again after that, just answered her monotone questions as personably as he could.

When she finally confirmed the discrepancy, he said, "Right. That's why I'm calling. I was really sick at the time, and I had someone else do my taxes. This is all a big misunderstanding. Just tell me what I owe, and I'll get a check in the mail today."

"I'm sorry, Mr. Murray, but that isn't possible. The audit is already underway. There will be—"

"But that's what I'm trying to tell you; there's no need for the audit because I can just take care of the discrepancy right now, over the phone."

"That's not the way it works, Mr. Murray," she repeated his name without a flicker of sympathy.

"So that's it? I don't get a chance to prove my case?"

"That's what the audit is for, Mr. Murray. The IRS is aware of the discrepancy, and fees have been assessed. Now the auditor will dig deeper to see if there's anything they missed. You'll have a chance to present additional evidence later in the process."

Later, after they'd decided he was guilty of tax evasion, and it would be ten times harder to sell a better story.

It was hard to pretend that it didn't piss him all the hell off being treated like a criminal. He'd spent the last year atoning for his mistakes with Paloma and Tyson. He shouldn't have to suffer through Julie's accusatory tone when he'd called to fix the problem.

A light rap on his door, then it cracked open, and

Angie slipped her head inside, making a gesture Nils couldn't understand. He shook his head, giving Angie a dirty look. Whatever it was, it could wait until he was done begging the IRS for mercy.

"What happens after the audit?" Nils asked Julie.

"A tax audit is performed to assess the validity and reliability of the information you have provided. The IRS may review your financial records, such as income statements, bank accounts, credit records, receipts, and monthly and annual expenditures."

It sounded like Julie was reading his eulogy.

And what the hell, Angie was already poking her head back inside, without knocking this time, making the same gesture again.

He swiveled his chair around, ignoring her.

"So, is there anything I can do to avoid this in the future?"

"Yes," Julie answered, so deadpan that Nils couldn't help but hear it as sarcasm, "make sure that what you make and what you report are the same numbers."

Nils thanked her before hanging up, even though she hadn't been helpful at all. Then there was anger for his father.

A man never stood as tall as when he kneeled to help his own child, but that was something Ed either didn't or couldn't understand.

Yes, he'd covered Nils's recovery, but that wasn't a gift so much as him finally paying a bill that was long overdue. The least his father could do, considering Ed was the reason he'd become an alcoholic in the first place.

Nils didn't just mean his genetic predisposition toward addiction, though that was a big deal. Ed had never once been willing to acknowledge the truth, going so far to roll his eyes as he called it a "bullshit excuse to help keep his son from manning up and admitting he'd lost control of himself."

Genetic predisposition wasn't a wild hair theory. There were a lot of family studies out there, including identical and fraternal twins or adopted children and siblings. Half a person's risk of developing a dependency on drugs or alcohol was linked to their genetic makeup. Ed didn't want to acknowledge that, not when it was so much easier to cast Nils as a "kid with arrested development, who refused to grow the hell up."

Maybe reporting Nils's income was Ed's way of getting him back. For the expense of rehab. Or the embarrassment of seeing his own alcoholism reflected back to him by his son.

Even now, after a lifetime of disappointment, Nils kept expecting his dad to do something different. But at this point, it was clear that Ed wasn't capable of change. So really, Nils was the problem. His father was only doing what he'd always done. Nils was the one expecting things to be different, either unwilling or unable to acknowledge the evidence and accept the reality.

He closed his eyes and leaned back in his chair, half-expecting the door to open the second he did. For Angie to poke her head in with more of her unnecessary and interruptive bullshit. It was irresponsible, her coming to work sick. She should have stayed home and kept her disgusting cough syrup with her.

And dammit. Now Nils was thinking about that bottle in a way that was frankly embarrassing. He used to have plenty of contempt for the folks in AA who told stories about drinking cough syrup when they couldn't get their hands on alcohol. But thinking about the bottle on Angie's desk right now, Nils could easily imagine himself taking a big swig, just enough to calm himself.

The thought made him shudder.

He was better than that.

But was he? Because Nils was also thinking about margaritas and had been for most of the morning. Now he wondered if there was such a thing as margarita-flavored cough syrup and what it might taste like if there was. Could there be a market for something like that?

Shit. He really needed to get out of here. The place had a way of slowly killing him, but today was worse than usual. He needed to get out of the office.

Nils opened his eyes and looked at his watch. Almost eleven. He would have to leave for lunch and get to The Cooling Rack for Tyson's cake soon.

He just had to get through the afternoon. Then he'd be on his way to the perfect evening: Tyson's birthday, the meeting where he'd get his one-year chip, and a romantic evening with Paloma, complete with flowers, chocolates, and an emerald pendant she'd cherish forever.

After a year of penance and sacrifice, he'd earned the right to a normal life again.

Except — Paloma was already planning another life for her and Tyson. How could he convince her that was a mistake?

What if she demanded more proof that he deserved to be her husband?

Then, a brilliant idea that would change everything.

Chapter Seven

TWO-FOR-ONE

Nils smiled at the banker.

The banker didn't smile back.

Either this dude was having a bad day, or he had so little laughter in his everyday life that the absence of merriment had withered his face. Nils looked at the banker's nameplate as he typed: *Ebon Bledsoe.*

Nils looked out the window at Cuchillo y Tenedor, the Mexican restaurant across the street. Advertising two-for-one margaritas. He swallowed, mouth watering, and forced his eyes back to the paper-strewn desk.

He wasn't here to have a margarita. He was here to be Paloma's hero.

But he couldn't stop tasting lime with a hint of salt or imagining how amazing a giant plate of nachos would taste after the tequila hit his system.

Ebon finished typing and looked up at Nils. "What was the amount you wanted to apply for?"

"The owner is asking for a million." He offered the banker yet another smile.

But Ebon didn't take it. He glanced at the empty chair beside Nils instead.

Ed could probably get more for the house, but the online calculator Nils had used to estimate what he'd qualify for had topped at just under seven figures.

But once he convinced Paloma, she'd have no problem talking his father down on the price.

Ebon gave Nils another arid look. "I'm sorry, Mr. Murray, but considering your income, your credit score, and your lack of a down payment, the most we could give you is a loan amount of $346,784."

Barely a third of what he actually needed. What bullshit.

"That's such a precise number. Why?" Nils sounded more accusatory than he'd intended. But it was too late to take it back.

"It's a formula, Mr. Murray, nothing personal."

But Ebon's expression said it might actually be.

"What's my credit score?" Nils asked.

A glance at his screen, then, "Well under six hundred."

"What would I need to get the loan?"

"Something substantially better."

"Obviously," Nils said, closer to snapping. "But what does that mean?"

"That I cannot qualify you for a million-dollar mortgage."

"You know what—" Nils shifted in his seat and leaned forward. If the man couldn't be charmed, maybe he could be moved to sympathy. "—I should've put my wife on the application. We'll be covering the mortgage together. Can we run the numbers again, but adding her income to the mix?"

Ebon looked at the empty seat again before returning

his disdain to Nils. "Your wife would need to sign the application before I could run it."

He added, "Unfortunately," even though he obviously didn't think it was.

Nils didn't understand the man's quiet hostility. But when he'd worked in sales, he'd countered ruffled feathers by calmly sticking to the facts. Maybe that would work here.

"We don't need to run the application. I just need a hypothetical, so my wife and I can discuss the numbers."

"Very well," said Ebon in a monotone. "What is her present income?"

Now they were getting somewhere.

Except that he wasn't exactly sure how much Paloma was making right now. She'd been promoted once, and hadn't she mentioned a raise a few months ago?

Ebon entered Nils's guess after an incredulous, and perhaps even cynical, glance.

"I'm sorry, Mr. Murray." He obviously wasn't. "But even with your combined incomes, these numbers still don't come close to qualifying for the loan amount you're requesting."

The banker offered him a *you're welcome* look, clearly waiting for Nils to thank him and leave in defeat.

But he wasn't going anywhere. Not without a much better answer. He owed it to Paloma and Tyson.

"Maybe there's still *something* we can do?" Nils said to Ebon with a buoyant expression, his voice kind and hopeful, his eyes as appreciative as he could possibly make them. "Maybe this is a problem we can pass forward, or kick up the line, or whatever we need to do?"

Ebon let out a long sigh, making Nils feel like a kindergartener about to get scolded by his teacher. "It is critical that a borrower be able to afford their loan."

"I understand. That's why I'm here. But check my history, I've never been late with rent or mortgage payments."

He was pretty sure Paloma would've kept up the payments on their old house. And that Ed would've helped her out if she'd needed it.

"The bank's decision will always come down to the numbers. Your existing obligations—"

"But it's my low credit score making the loan numbers so high, right? If I had perfect credit, my interest would be lower, and so would the payments. Maybe—"

"We could look past a less-than-ideal credit score if you're buying a house within your means."

Now Ebon was being insulting. "How do you know what is or isn't in my means?"

"Keeping your debt-to-income ratio below—"

"I just need someone to understand," Nils started, hating that he had to humble himself but willing to do it if it saved their home. "We did rack up a lot of debt, but that's only because I had a medical condition. I'm recovering, but we've had a really rough year. My family is about to get kicked out of our house. We've been given six weeks to vacate."

Finally, a flicker of sympathy on Ebon's face. If he'd known this was what it would take, he'd have started here.

He hit the closer hard. "My son is about to turn six. It's his birthday today. I can't go home and tell him that we're going to be homeless. *Please*, isn't there anything you can do to help us out?"

Nils actually held his breath as the banker tapped at his keyboard for a few moments. The printer in the corner started spitting pages, which Ebon collected and set in front of him.

But the top sheet didn't contain mortgage terms or contract language. It was a real estate listing.

"There's a bank foreclosure auction coming up." Ebon actually looked pleased with himself. "With your wife's income, you'll have no trouble finding a new home."

Nils could feel dismay souring his expression but was unable to stop it. "A foreclosed piece of property? You mean a dump."

"Not all foreclosed properties are distressed, Mr. Murray." Ebon cleared his throat. "Sometimes families fall on hard times or buy something beyond their means, despite how careful we are to screen for that. But yes, you are correct, foreclosures often need a lot of fixing up. I imagine that's still better than being homeless."

Nils wanted to reach across the desk, grab Ebon by his tie, and choke him until he apologized for spending the last twenty minutes silently judging him.

"Would you like to work on the pre-qualification now?"

"No." Nils was on his feet, angry and quickly getting angrier. He'd held it in long enough. If he didn't get out of there right now, he would explode. "Thank you so very, very much."

He didn't wait for Ebon's response, and as he hurried out of the bank, Nils felt his glare like spiders crawling on his back. It took all of his willpower to avoid the relief he'd surely find in two-for-one margaritas across the street.

Paloma would laugh in his face if he proposed that they pool their resources to buy some shitty foreclosure. It would be one more sign of his failure to get his life on track in time.

Ed's fault for pulling the rug out from under Nils before he was ready.

He didn't deserve any of this.

He turned the engine, but before he pulled out of his parking spot, he looked longingly at the hand-painted sign, tasting the margarita on his tongue.

Two of them, for the price of one.

Today was exactly the kind of day that had made Nils start drinking in the first place. It was bad enough that people were the way they were; he shouldn't have to worry about losing his family.

Not after everything he'd done to win them back.

He pulled out of the parking lot, making a right instead of a left to avoid driving by Cuchillo y Tenedor.

But a change in direction didn't stop him from craving margaritas.

He licked his lips. Imagined the salted rim of a chilled glass.

Sipping the tart, icy liquid.

Feeling the tequila warming him from inside and burning his frustration away.

Then he swallowed, dying for a drink.

Nils pulled over. He was seconds from making a U-turn he couldn't afford. He would stay here until he no longer wanted to drown himself in margaritas.

If only he could call Jakob.

No, that would be admitting defeat. Nils wasn't weak. He just needed a reminder.

So he pulled out his chip and stared at it. Tonight he would trade eleven months for a full year. Then everything would be different. He just needed to get through this one last day to have everything he ever wanted.

He spied the glowing promise of a different vice ahead in the distance.

Then floored the gas and roared toward it.

Chapter Eight

STOPPING AT SLOPPY'S

SLOPPY'S WAS the worst fast food joint in the world. And the best.

Nils looked down at his burger. He couldn't let The True American get cold because then it would be disgusting. It was a steaming pile of hedonism cobbled together from cheap, highly-processed ingredients imbued with the kind of intense flavors that only sophisticated chemistry could create.

His mouth was going to love it. Worth the flaming shits for sure. Nils was going to stuff himself until he felt sick. Something he'd done often during his first couple months after getting out of rehab. Eating until he was overcome with greasy nausea killed his desire to drink.

He wasn't any different from Crissy, only his choice of distractions.

He didn't want to drink and was damn close to doing something much worse to his body and mind than mowing through a True American, with four different artificial cheeses and a sauce that was probably "special" because it was mostly MSG.

He popped a handful of fries into his mouth and unwrapped his burger while chewing. Hot and salty, crispy on the outside, and fluffy on the inside. Did it make a difference that he could leave those fries on the counter and come back to them two weeks later, and they would look exactly the same? Not to him. Not right now.

He bit into his burger and smiled.

Ranch squirted into both sides of his mouth. Flavor tested and perfected for the bastardized American palate. The place knew exactly what it was doing.

Another bite, better than before. Fuck the documentaries. Nils had seen them. The processed food in their factories, cruelties on their farms, and astronomical calorie counts.

The only thing that mattered now was how fast he could fill the hole inside him with this burger.

He gulped down a mouthful of his Twinkie shake (with chunks of real Twinkie blended into the frozen hydrogenated oils and sugar).

He loved it, even though it made him hate himself a little bit more.

Nils kept chewing, looking around at all the other losers like him. The girl with the nose ring? Nils guessed she was trapped in a relationship she should have already fled. What was keeping her there? Shame? Loyalty? Something worse? For the next six or seven minutes, the Impossibly Delicious in her hand would feel like her very best friend in the world.

The man sitting in the nearest booth looked like he was trying to eat himself to death. He'd arranged a smorgasbord of sides around his Kitchen Sink Stacker. The Mixer, a double-large sleeve crammed with seasoned fries and onion rings with garlic butter dipping sauce. A box of bright red Szechuan Crispies (technically a form of chicken nuggets and Szechuan in color only). And for dessert, a Blue Betty huckleberry pie whose filling was probably more cornstarch and food coloring than actual berries.

If he didn't get his shit together, these would be his people.

Nils looked longingly at his final bite, not wanting to eat it. Every mouthful was perfect, and in moments it would be gone. But for right now, in these waning seconds, Sloppy's was nirvana.

He took a deep breath and shoved the last bite into his mouth.

There was a time when even this wouldn't have been enough to keep him away from the booze. In his early days of sobriety, he'd go back for an Impossibly Delicious and eat until he was so full it hurt to breathe.

Back in the car, Nils caught a glimpse of the dashboard clock, and his heart wanted to stop. Twelve-fifteen. He'd wasted too much time with Ebon. Now he'd have to rush to the bakery.

Of course, traffic was a nightmare.

Of course, everyone on the road was driving like an asshole.

And of course, he was stuck behind some idiot in a Porsche Cayenne who couldn't pick a lane.

Another red light.

Another idiot in front of him.

Another panic attack threatening Nils with the reality that he might not get to The Cooling Rack in time. After Paloma had made such a big fucking deal about picking up the cake. Why hadn't he gone to the bakery first?

Because Crissy and Ebon and Angie and all the other idiots in his life made him want to drown himself in tequila.

He changed lanes, then switched back to the right, same as that asshole in the Cayenne.

He glanced over at the woman in the older Honda Accord beside him. She shook her head, shooting him a withering look. Nils felt bad, but not enough to miss his chance.

He accelerated into the opening and changed lanes again, getting in front of the Accord and giving the woman a wave as he did it, looking up into his rearview and meeting her glare.

Sorry, he mouthed to himself.

If he could get to the bakery before they closed, then the risks he was taking would be worth it. He couldn't fail to get the cake.

The stop-and-go refused to get faster. Nils wasn't a smoker and hadn't even picked up the habit while battling sobriety like some addicts did. But right now, his fingers were twitching for a cigarette, just so he'd have something to do while trapped in this purgatory of traffic.

This congestion was representative of everything else that had gone wrong with his day so far. It was as though the universe itself was working to keep Nils from properly restarting his life. Everyone was trying to steal his fresh start, to sabotage his efforts so it would look like he'd barely even tried.

But Nils had spent the last year doing nothing but trying. He was exhausted from trying. And still, it hadn't been enough for Paloma. Her ultimatum stood: a year of sobriety to prove his permanent change.

Another lane, back and forth, and Nils was just like that asshole in the Cayenne.

As if the thought had summoned him, the Cayenne's driver came out of nowhere to cut Nils off again.

He eased up, no choice really, and let the SUV slip in

front of him. Another glance at the clock, then at his watch, in case the numbers disagreed. They didn't, and now he was white-knuckling the steering wheel.

The Cayenne didn't make it through the light before it turned red, and neither did Nils. If the dickhead hadn't cut in front of him, he would have had enough momentum to make it through that last light.

Now he wouldn't get to the bakery to pick up Tyson's cake. His son would be disappointed, and Paloma would be furious.

Nils could accept the consequences of his actions, no problem; that's what AA was all about. But it killed him that he'd be getting in trouble for nothing. Nothing he'd done, anyway.

He kept breathing, still wishing for a cigarette as the light turned green, and he accelerated through it.

Traffic cleared on the other side. He pressed down on the gas with a swell of hope, stealing a few more miles per hour. The Cayenne was flying, with Nils soaring just behind it. He'd been lucky to hit 20 MPH before, but now he was at 30, 35, 45 … more.

The Cooling Rack was ahead, just on the other side of the light. Nils might be saved if he kept going. But the light turned yellow — not a problem with the Cayenne sailing through it.

Nils hit the gas, desperate to make it through on the yellow.

But the Cayenne slammed on its brakes at the last second, apparently deciding the light would turn red before it could get through and that the risk wasn't worth it. By the time Nils stomped on his own brakes, it was too late.

He couldn't switch lanes, cars were hugging him from either side, so he braced for the worst and got it.

Brakes squealed like banshees in battle as he slowed. It was almost enough. He nearly made it, but some sort of bullshit astral interference had been fucking with his shit all day, and Fate apparently felt like it needed to fuck with him even harder.

Even though he slowed enough that Nils was only going a few miles an hour, he still crashed into the back of the Cayenne, cursing himself, the universe, and the idiot driver in front of him, pounding both fists onto the steering wheel and involuntarily roaring into the cabin.

Nils waited through what felt like the longest light of his life, then put on his blinkers and pulled over to the side of the road right behind the Cayenne, spitting distance from the bakery.

The driver was already out of the Cayenne before Nils could put his own car in Park. She looked furious. Severe raven hair with sharp bangs, and ends so trim she must have had them cut just an hour ago. Tall, thin, and determined, her anger swelling as she marched over toward him.

"Do you not know what yellow means?" she yelled.

"I'm sorry." Nils raised his hands in surrender. "I didn't mean to—"

"You weren't paying attention."

"I know, that's what I'm trying to say, but—"

"But nothing. You rear-ended me. That means the accident is your fault."

"I'm not arguing that." Nils drew a breath. He was taking responsibility, so why was she so immediately hostile? "I was in too much of a hurry, and I'm sorry. It's because—"

"I don't care *why* you hit me, sir. I only care that—"

"My name is Nils. You can—"

"Why don't you finish introducing yourself with insurance and registration?" She brandished her own and held them out for him to take. "We should trade this before we call the police."

"Whoa, wait a minute." Again he raised his hands. "Why do we need to call the police?"

"Because there's been an accident," she said, as though Nils were an imbecile.

He glanced at her bumper. "I understand that, but there's barely any damage and—"

"The amount of damage doesn't matter, sir—"

"Nils."

"—it matters that there was an accident."

"Only if there's injury or death," he argued.

"Or damage exceeding a thousand dollars."

"It's only a scratch."

The woman said nothing, staring into his stupidity instead.

Nils tried again. "Insurance can take care of this, *please*. I really need to—"

"All drivers of any vehicles involved in an accident are required by California law to report the accident to their local police department within twenty-four hours of the crash. Right now is the best time to do that."

Nils shook his head and pointed to The Cooling Rack. "I need to get over to that bakery *right now*. They close in a few minutes. If you want to follow me over there, I'd be happy to—"

"You need to calm down, sir."

"Stop calling me, sir. And I'm trying to be reasonable, but you're—"

"It isn't just important that we comply with the law, anything we report now can be used as evidence in an insurance claim or lawsuit later."

"A lawsuit?"

"It's important to take action as soon as possible following the event of an accident."

This woman was a goddamned hall monitor.

He smiled, hoping that might help. "Look, I hear everything you're saying. And I agree that we should file a police report." He didn't. "But I really need to get across the street. So—"

"You're welcome to leave. But I'm filing a police report, and if you go anywhere, then I'll have to request that they charge you with a hit-and-run."

"You've gotta be kidding me." Nils threw his hands in the air. This was unbelievable. But he softened his voice, a move he'd learned while pacifying Paloma. "I'm really sorry I rear-ended you. I wasn't paying attention, and it's all my fault. Because—"

"I don't care why you hit me."

"—today is my son's sixth birthday, and I promised my wife that I'd pick up the cake. They're closing right now, and traffic was terrible. I—"

"Didn't properly plan for your day?" she finished.

"I'm sorry, what was your name?"

Instead of answering, the woman offered him her insurance again. He didn't want to take it, knowing there was defeat in acceptance. But he took it because sometimes you won by losing.

Gloria, read the insurance card.

"Gloria, please don't make me disappoint my son. I can get the cake and come right back if you—"

"The cars shouldn't be—"

"Oh my God!" Nils yelled. "Can you please stop being a fucking robot for five minutes?"

"Is that how you ask for a favor?"

This was absurd. Fate still having her way with him.

"Fine. Call the cops," Nils said through gritted teeth, then told his phone, "Dial *The Cooling Rack*."

"Cooling Rack," answered a man who sounded baked as a cake.

"I know you guys are closing, but—"

"You can't make it by one, but you need your cake, *riiight?*"

"You must get this a lot," Nils said, watching Gloria call the police.

"All the time, man. We'll be here fifteen, maybe twenty minutes longer. Could be more if Mario has one of his dick cakes in the oven. Let me put it this way: we'll probably be here, but we ain't waiting."

The line went dead.

Nils swallowed hard, tried to convince himself to call Paloma and ask if she could please pick up the cake. But he couldn't do it. That would be admitting his failure, and she would never take him back if he ruined two of his son's birthday parties in a row.

But there was someone he could call.

"What's up?" Crissy answered immediately, sounding surprised yet happy to hear from him.

"I need a favor."

"Anything." A giggle, then, "For reals."

"Do you know where The Cooling Rack is?"

"What's that?"

"A bakery. On Studebaker and Cross."

"Oh, sure. You want to meet there?"

"I can't. That's the problem. I'm supposed to pick up Tyson's cake, but the place closes at one, but they said they'd be hanging around for a few more minutes. And I just got into an accident. So—"

"I'll be right down, then I'll wait in the parking lot until you get here."

"I'm so sorry, but the favor's even bigger than that. I'm stupid late for work, and I need to get something important done before five. Would it be possible for you to bring the cake by my office?"

"I have an even better idea. I'm already in the car — I'll take your cake home and put it in the fridge. You can pick it up on your way home from work. I'll text you the address."

Nils could finally exhale. "You're a lifesaver. Really. Thanks, times a million."

"Least I could do."

"Thanks. Again. I'll see you after work." He hung up, feeling a ray of hope for his day, despite Gloria grinning in victory a few feet away.

Nils prayed that Mario was making a dick cake and that he had yet to stick it in the oven.

Chapter Nine

SO BE IT

EITHER NILS HAD LEFT his office door open, or someone was waiting for him.

Shit. When he checked his calendar this morning, the afternoon had been clear. Had Angie scheduled him for something but forgotten to block off the time?

He stepped inside, and it was worse than he'd thought. Janice Schultz — head of HR and his immediate supervisor — leaned against his desk. One of the company lawyers, Louis Something, stood beside her, arms crossed. Both looked like they'd been sucking on a lemon rind.

Nils nodded at them as he entered. Neither of them nodded back.

"Did you tell Stew that the company would cover his rehab?" Janice asked.

Without taking his seat, Nils said, "I did."

"Why on earth would you do that?" Louis managed to make it sound less like a question and more like an insult.

The way Janice watched him made Nils feel like he was one wrong response from unemployment.

A breath before he answered. "Under section 8.14 in the policy handbook—"

"He can't go to rehab," Louis said.

"Company policy says he can," Nils replied.

Janice's lips flattened into a severe line. Why wasn't she sticking up for him? She knew the policy better than he did.

Louis said, "If he starts rehab, then we won't be able to let him go until after he's finished with his six-month probationary period."

"To give him a chance to prove himself."

"He doesn't deserve a chance to prove himself, and he sure as hell isn't getting one. Stew Boyer needs to be terminated immediately."

Janice finally spoke, delivering her missive without a hint of emotion. "I get the feeling that you don't understand what's happening here."

"I guess not." Nils neglected to add, *I thought I was doing my job.*

Louis said, "You were supposed to fire him, not give the guy a hug."

"Since when do we not issue warnings and give employees a chance to correct their mistakes?"

Louis scoffed. "Since Stew did something to seriously jeopardize the future of Ember Chemical."

That sounded like an overstatement. "He knows he's been sloppy, and there are mitigating—"

"Why do you think I sent Stew into your office?" Louis asked.

"Because he'd been caught drinking at work. I know that's bad, but it isn't a fireable offense. Which is why I suggested rehab. We can—"

"He sent proprietary information to one of our

competitors," Janice said, still in a monotone. "Trinity Global."

Louis nodded. "Corporate espionage is grounds for immediate termination and legal action. Ember will be pursuing both."

Stew had fucked him, pretending to be the victim when he must have known he'd done something wrong. "Believe me, I had no idea."

"Then you should've checked with his supervisor," Louis snapped. "Because it's *your job* to know."

None of this was his fault. Stew's supervisor, Wilkes, should have spoken to Nils directly before sending Stew to him. And where was Angie in all this? She was supposed to keep him apprised of the situation.

And if this was such a big deal, why hadn't Janice fired him? Or Louis?

Why me?

The question that seemed to be defining his day.

Ignoring Louis, he turned to Janice and said, "I'm happy to fix my mistake, and I do understand how serious this is, but seeing as how I already messed up this morning in a way that made Stew believe I was sympathetic to his situation, wouldn't it be better if someone else were to let him go?"

"This is your job, Nils. If you can't do it, I can't keep you on in this position."

"Make it fast," Louis chimed in. "A security guard is on the way up to escort him from the building."

Nils wiped a half cup of sweat from his palms onto his pants, then picked up the phone and ordered Angie to call Stew in immediately. Then he told Janice, "I'll let you know when it's taken care of."

"We'll know it's taken care of when we see you take care of it."

Nils wondered if Janice was sick of Louis speaking for her yet. Or if that was just part of *her* job, putting up with arrogant dickheads.

They waited in silence while Nils sat at his desk and tried not to fidget.

When Stew arrived, he vented a nervous laugh. "So, is this rehab getting started?"

Without any preamble or even an *I'm sorry*, Nils said, "Effective immediately, Ember Chemical is terminating your contract."

"What?"

Nils steeled himself against the shock and betrayal on Stew's face. "Leaking proprietary information is grounds for immediate termination."

Stew stared back at him blankly.

The peanut gallery wasn't about to help him out, so Nils added, "We know about your email to Trinity."

"You know I have a problem!" Stew blurted. "You said you understood. You promised that the company would pay for rehab and that I would get another chance!"

"Nils should have known better than to promise you anything without having a conversation about it with me first."

That came from Janice, and it woke new fear in Nils. So far, it seemed like she'd understood he'd made an honest mistake.

Nils swallowed. "I'm sorry for raising your hopes, Stew. I didn't have all the information. And to be fair, you didn't tell me the truth."

"I told you what you asked." Stew was sweating, his face flushed. "You didn't ask me about the email."

"But you knew you were being called in for a reprimand, at the very least. And you knew you'd sent the email."

"Isn't there anything I can do?" Stew begged. "I'm sorry, I swear. Anything?"

"Security is waiting downstairs to escort you off the—"

Nils didn't even get to finish with *premises*. Stew shot to his feet and swept a wild arm across the desk, knocking Nils's family picture onto the floor.

"FUCK ALL OF YOU!" Stew marched out the door, looked back over his shoulder to add, "ESPECIALLY YOU, NILS!"

"Asshole," Louis muttered under his breath.

"Very professional," she shot back at the lawyer. "Thank you for your assistance."

"Where were you?" Janice asked once Louis was gone.

"You mean while you were all waiting in my office?" Nils answered, trying not to sound irritated, despite the interrogation he didn't deserve. "I was at lunch."

"Angie said you left for lunch before eleven, and you didn't make it back here until almost two." She waited for Nils to respond, then finished when he didn't. "Are you regularly in the habit of taking nearly three hours for lunch?"

"No, ma'am. I was in a traffic accident and had to stay until the police arrived."

"I'm sure there's a police report to support your story?"

It wasn't really a question, but Nils was thrilled he could nod to it anyway. *Thanks, Gloria.* "Absolutely."

"Angie tells me that you're out of the office a lot. Do you always get into traffic accidents during lunch?"

"No, ma'am." Nils bristled at the implication that he was lying about why he'd been late. "Just today."

"Being in the HR department like you are, what would you say to an employee in your situation right now?"

"What situation?"

"An employee taking off from work whenever they feel like it, irrespective of their responsibilities."

"I don't take time off of work whenever I feel like it."

"Just the three hours for today?"

"Part of that was for lunch," Nils tried to argue, immediately regretting the words as they left him.

"So you only stole two hours from Ember today, is that what you're saying?"

"No, I just had to stay until the police could look at my car—"

"Don't worry about it, Nils. You can make up the two hours today, and we'll call it even starting tomorrow. Meaning, I'll be checking in to make sure that this never happens again."

"I understand, and I hear you. But please, today is my son's birthday—"

"Are you asking to leave early, too?"

"No, ma'am."

"Don't give Louis another reason to show up in my office, Nils."

"I won't, ma'am."

But as he watched her leave, Nils wasn't sure he could keep that promise.

Because this was the most important night of his life. He couldn't let anyone take that away from him. Not Janice, not Louis, and definitely not that snitch Angie.

Tonight, he was getting *normal* back.

If they wanted to fire him for doing right by his family, so be it.

Chapter Ten

EARNED TRUST

To do his job well, Nils had to be wise. But today, he'd shown no wisdom at all.

He exhaled in a huff and turned to his computer. The churning in his stomach made it feel like he really had eaten the shit pie he still felt between his metaphorical teeth. Nothing was worse than fucking up in front of an audience.

He should've been hacking through those workers' comp forms, but instead, he sought a few moments of escape. He started with Abode, a real estate site that let you look up the approximate value of any home. He plugged in his father's address and clicked *Estimate the Abode*. One-point-three million. Worse than he'd thought.

But that was an estimate. If Paloma asked Ed, he might agree to lower the price. Especially if she neglected to mention that she was asking on Nils's behalf as well.

He clicked away to Forage. *Best online mortgage*, he typed into the search engine.

That took him to Fundid. They were the third result, but Nils liked that they "made getting an online mortgage fun." It was by no means a party, but Fundid had gone out of the way to make everything easy by summarizing the legalese in human-speak underneath every question.

Nils needed something simple, especially since he was dying to drink. He'd gone from imagining a dalliance with margaritas to a one-night stand with shots of tequila.

Thank goodness he'd started a company-hosted AA group about six months ago, so he could help his fellow employees whose lunch hours didn't allow them enough time to attend an offsite meeting. He'd sold it to Janice as an additional HR program that cost nothing but his time, although really, he'd been high on the encouragement from sharing his insights with others in recovery and had been looking for another place to do that.

He'd never imagined needing the group to keep *him* on track.

But he had half an hour before they met and was determined to buy his father's house. If he could make it through an entire year without drinking, he could find a way to pull this off. An online application would let him use Paloma's info, plugging her income into his without requiring a physical signature.

Maybe a lender like Fundid would be more relaxed about all the niggling little rules that traditional banks obsessed over.

On the final screen, Fundid asked him which he preferred, the question in an oversized Helvetica above a trio of pictures: balloons, fireworks, or — no shit — what looked like margaritas.

It didn't count if they were virtual, right?

He clicked on the drinks, and words appeared on the screen.

Drinks are on us while we see how much we can fund you!

An animation appeared. Two margaritas getting filled

by a pair of magnificent-looking pitchers. The glasses were then raised by two invisible hands and emptied into invisible mouths on either side.

Then the animation replayed and replayed again. A few more times.

Nils turned his head away until a shift in brightness told him that the screen had reloaded.

He eventually turned back to study his rejection. Approved for not quite half of what he needed to buy his father's house.

Today was supposed to be special. Instead, it had been an avalanche of catastrophe.

He needed that meeting.

For a year, Nils had dealt with every blow that came his way, and all without a single drink. But now he was running on empty. The world was piling on top of him. He didn't just want something to take the edge off, he was dying to get drunk. A margarita wouldn't do, and to hell with the pitcher. He wanted a bottle of tequila.

No, drunk wouldn't cut it. Nils wanted to be legless, trousered, and trolleyed; hammered beyond recognition. He could wake up when it was all over and try this thing again.

But that was just bullshit from the loser inside him. He'd taught himself to ignore the voice. He did that now, clicking out of Fundid and navigating into less savory options. Scammy-looking websites promising him the house of his dreams, no matter what his credit score. Nils just had to enter a few bits of personal information, and his mortgage was guaranteed.

He didn't, of course, but it depressed him that the only options left to him were, at best, an opportunity to sign up for spam and, at worst, probably identity theft operations that preyed on the desperate.

There was only one humiliating thing he could think of to try. But given how his day had gone so far, he might as well suck it up and embarrass himself again.

He took out his phone and dialed his father.

"Nils," Ed said over a cacophony in the background. "What's up?"

Nils heard a riot of laughter and voices. "I wanted to talk to you about something."

"Now?"

"That is when I'm calling."

A long pause, then, "Well, get on with it."

"Are you at the VFW right now?"

"What does it matter to you? Just say whatever you need to say."

Curses in the background like balls in a game. Of course, he was at the V.F.W., drinking with his buddies. "I wanted to make you an offer. On the house."

His father scoffed. "You can't afford my house."

"It's my house, too."

"It isn't your house at all."

"I grew up in it."

"You also grew up in California. Do you own that?" Ed laughed.

"That's not even remotely the same, and you know it. But you're right. I can't afford your house. I went to the bank for a loan because I'd like to buy it, but I could only get approved for half of what it's worth."

"Sounds about right," said Ed. Like an asshole.

"What I can get approved for isn't the same as what I can afford," Nils argued. "I can make higher payments and cover the difference under the table."

Nils could hear his father drinking. He swallowed too, thinking longingly of the tequila he could not under any circumstances allow himself to have.

"In my experience, what you can get approved for and what you can afford are generally the same exact thing. And second—" Ed took another sip, "—what you're suggesting is illegal."

"Seriously, Dad? *Illegal?* We're family. Are you really telling me that this is something you can't do for your son because it doesn't follow the letter of the law? Since when did you ever give a shit about that?"

"Don't swear at me, son. Especially when you're asking for a favor."

It was getting louder in the background and harder to hear.

Nils kept suffering from the wrong kind of thirst.

He took a breath before speaking again. "I'm offering to pay you the full amount."

"Which you can't afford."

"Maybe not right away, but you know I'm good for it. And besides, all the extra money is under the table."

"It's not *extra money* if it's part of the purchase price. But more to the point, paying it under the table is illegal."

"You're seriously still on that?" Nils licked his lips. "It doesn't matter that we're family?"

"You're living in my guest house right now, aren't you?"

"Only because of Tyson."

"You might be right." Ed started drinking again, finishing this time with a satisfied sigh.

Nils was glad he was stuck at the office while his dad was getting sloshed in the same bar where he'd spent too much of his son's childhood. Because right now, he was pissed enough to throw punches.

"That's fair. I did more than a few things to damage our relationship and your trust in me. But we can work this out. Just treat the loan like a bank would. I fall three months behind in my payments to you, the house is yours to—"

"Deal with? No, thank you."

"Can you please just—"

"This is a conversation you should be having with Paloma."

"I need to know that I can make it happen first."

His father paused again, his longest so far, and this time it didn't sound like he was filling the silence with a drink. "I don't think Paloma's on board with buying a house right now, at least not with you."

Nils inhaled and exhaled, ignoring the heat on his neck, clammy hands, and overstrained heart. He ignored the rage, welling like a tornado kicking a tumbleweed before turning into fury itself.

He swallowed, then softly said, "What if you co-signed on a loan with us for the full amount?"

"You're not listening. Paloma—"

"It's the least you can do for abandoning us."

Another long pause, but this time Nils noticed that the background was silent. Had Ed put him on speakerphone? So that all of his drunk buddies could listen in while he humiliated his son?

"I'm not abandoning anyone, Nils. And since you've been indulging yourself without listening to dick for the entirety of this phone call, I guess I'll have to try something else."

"What do you mean?"

"You just got your life together. Why commit yourself to a mortgage you can't afford? Don't you understand how easy it'll be to derail all the progress you've made?"

Nils *just* got his life together?

"I've been sober for a year, and I know what I can handle."

"I'm not sure you do," Ed disagreed.

It was still mostly silent on his father's side. Nils could hear passing traffic in the distance, and maybe a bird.

"So even after a year, I've still done nothing to earn your trust?"

"You've done plenty to earn my trust."

"Then why won't you even consider—"

"You're asking to borrow twice what the bank will allow when you're going on three months late with me. Seriously, son, what did you expect?"

For the fucker to acknowledge that Nils had changed and stop treating him like the irresponsible jackass he used to be. Was that too much to ask?

Nils glanced at the clock. Just a few minutes left until his meeting. It was going to take every shred of willpower to get off the elevator at the third floor instead of heading all the way down to the lobby, then out the door and into the first bar in sight.

He took a breath and tried one more time.

"All I want is for you to treat me like a grownup instead of the fuckup kid you keep thinking I am."

"Then you should understand exactly how I feel because that's all I want, too."

"That's not even—"

"Not this time, Nils. The house is sold, the deal is done. There's no point in trying to change my mind. Even if it wasn't already sold, there's zero chance that I'd sell it to you. It's not personal, though I can see why you'd have a hard time believing that. But even if you could land a big enough loan, there are things you need to work out with your wife first."

"What do you know about it?"

"More than you, apparently."

"I can't believe this. I can't believe that you won't help your own son."

"I've always helped you, Nils. And I still will if you'll stop being a self-indulgent asshole. There are plenty of ways I can offer you a hand without giving you a handout."

"You're not giving me a handout."

"You can try that again when you don't owe me rent."

"You're kicking us out into the street so you can retire to fucking Florida."

"Paloma didn't have a problem with the news. She just gave me a hug and made me promise that I wouldn't start cooking meth and wrestling alligators."

Nils snorted.

"Are we done? Can I hang up the phone and get back inside to my friends without getting accused of abandoning you?"

"Sorry, your son has emotional needs. It must suck to have someone constantly reaching out to you for love and affection."

"Relationships are a two-way street, Nils."

Ed hung up.

Nils dropped his phone onto the desk and clenched his fists several times before wiping them on his pants.

He stood and paced the small office, making himself dizzy enough to collapse back in his chair.

He spun around several times, his throat getting drier and drier, screaming for a drink.

Nils got back up, still dizzy but willing to walk if it meant he'd make his meeting.

He left his office, spying the cough syrup, but avoiding Angie's curious eyes.

Down to the employee lounge, where he could talk about drinking.

Hand in his pocket, squeezing the chip, strong at 365 proof.

He pressed it into his palm until it hurt, distracting him so he might not dwell on his father.

But no, the thoughts came to drown him anyway.

And liquid memories made him crave a drink.

How dare Ed lecture him with more of his tough-love bullshit? He lost the right to play Augie Doggie and Doggy Daddy when he frittered his kid's teenage years away, getting plastered at the VFW. He liked comparing Nils to himself, but the comparison was bullshit. They were father and son, but completely unalike.

Damn straight, relationships were a two-way street.

If Ed understood what that actually meant, he'd have loaned Nils the money.

Hell, he'd have waited to sell the house until Nils could get the money on his own and let him keep his dignity.

And he'd have apologized for all the years he'd treated Nils like he didn't exist.

It didn't matter anymore. For most of his life, Nils had barely had a father. Soon Ed would be so far away, it would be the same as if he'd been orphaned.

Fine with him. Nils didn't need a father, as long as he could *be* a father.

He just had to get through this day without a drink.

Chapter Eleven

OVERRULED

THE GROUP usually lit up when he entered the room, despite the spoken agreement that they were all equals in recovery. Nils had been their de facto leader since he'd brought them together, hooking each one with his inspirational story and hard-won insights.

But today, they stayed huddled in their corner, talking in hushed whispers and failing to notice his arrival.

Until he cleared his throat.

All seven of them snapped around like they'd just been caught plotting a murder. Or maybe … planning a surprise party to celebrate his year of sobriety?

Maybe this was his day turning around, shifting from helter-skelter to hunky-dory. The world saying, *just kidding, I did all that so you wouldn't guess the real surprise.*

But before he could suggest they get started, Lacy stepped forward and asked, "Did you fire Stew?"

So much for his day turning around. How'd they find out so fast?

"I didn't want to, but it wasn't my call." Nils sighed so

they'd know how hard it had been for him. "I was just doing my job."

"Nuh-uh." Ike jabbed a finger at Nils. "No way, man. Your job is to support your brothers and sisters down here."

Then Lacy jumped in: "Stew said you tricked him into admitting he had a problem. Said you told him he could go to rehab and everything, then you used what he told you in confidence against him."

The whole group glared as one.

And Nils couldn't defend himself because he couldn't explain to them what Stew had done wrong. He'd be infringing on Stew's right to privacy, and that could open management up to a lawsuit.

"Look," Nils tried again. "There was nothing I could do. Believe me, I did my best. But Stew made a mistake, knowingly or not, that not only breached his employment contract, it verged into corporate espionage."

"Oh, is that the excuse you used to fire him?" Ike was working himself up into a rage. "I call bullshit. Stew was a good man."

"Ike, I swear—"

"I promised Stew he could trust you. 'Nils understands. He won't judge.' That's what I said to him."

"Stew's journey was already set before you suggested he talk to me." Calm, authoritative voice. Non-threatening gesture, palm outstretched. Just like Jakob used to do. "You did the right thing by encouraging him to reach out for help. He's taken the first step, admitting he has a problem and that he's not in control."

Ike snorted. "Any other clichés you wanna spit my way?"

"How can we trust you now?" Lacy asked, and for the

first time, Nils realized that this wasn't so much about Stew as it was about them. And him.

He needed to regain their trust. Which meant throwing Ember under the bus. Something he was never supposed to do as an HR rep.

But Ember had already thrown Nils under the bus, hadn't they?

"I'd already started the process of enrolling him in rehab—" a tiny lie that they had no way of verifying, "—when the head of HR overruled me."

But if this story got around, he didn't want it getting back to his boss that he'd blamed her. So he added, "She didn't have a choice either. Legal insisted that we fire him."

"There's always a choice," Ike said as he stood. "You decided that Stew wasn't worth sticking up for."

He pointedly turned his back on Nils before leaving the room.

Lacy huffed and followed Ike out the door.

And just like that, the meeting was over.

"Hey, remember when I sat up with you until three in the morning after Edgar left?" Nils asked Daniel's back. Then to Kate, "Didn't I pick you up at El Paso Cantina at midnight, after you backslid last month?"

Neither answered, and soon, only one person remained.

"Simon, right?" Nils asked.

The twenty-something from accounting had only joined last month, and he'd barely talked outside of admitting that he'd started binge-drinking in college with the frat brothers he so desperately missed.

At least he understood that Nils was only trying to help.

"Who's Stew?" Simon asked.

Nils shook his head and tried to make his face indifferent. "It doesn't matter, let's focus on you."

"Everyone seemed pretty upset about whatever that was."

"That's because they don't understand. Most people are just followers. Ike is the only one who has a real problem with what happened, but everyone likes him, so …"

"Maybe I should have followed them, too."

"Maybe we should get started," Nils said, attempting to redirect the conversation.

"Doesn't look like there'll be much of a meeting."

"There's two of us, that's enough for a meeting. What would you like to talk about?"

"Who's Stew?" Simon asked again.

Nils sighed. "An employee I had to fire today, against my wishes. I'm not at liberty to tell you what happened, but I can absolutely say that it was a fireable offense and that I was only doing my job. I went out on a limb for the guy, recommending him for rehab, and I got chewed out for it."

Simon seemed even more nervous than before. "He got fired after getting recommended for rehab?"

"No, it wasn't like that." Nils shook his head. "Rehab had nothing to do with it. I didn't know what Stew had actually done until after I came back from lunch."

"How could you not know what he'd done if you were the one in charge of firing him?"

"My assistant has been sick, she's been letting things slip through the cracks."

Simon looked incredulous. "Does the company track who comes to these meetings?"

"No. These meetings are employee-run and completely confidential."

The kid looked far from convinced. "But you run them. And you work for HR."

"Not in my capacity as an HR rep."

"My supervisor is a real straight-edge. He finds out I'm in AA, it'll affect my performance review." Simon jumped up.

"You're safe," Nils tried. "I promise."

"Sounds like a lot of promises get broken here."

Nils caught up to Simon at the door, putting a friendly hand on his shoulder. "Stay. Please. I want to help you."

"Can you help yourself? Sorry, but I'm outtie." With his hand on the doorknob, he turned back to Nils. "When you get back to your office, put it in my file that I've only gone to one meeting because now I'm cured."

Nils laughed in Simon's face. He didn't mean to, but— "You're never *cured*. You'll always be an alcoholic. AA is here to help you develop strategies for—"

Simon shook off Nils's hand and hurried into the hallway.

What if Simon was right?

What if he couldn't even help himself?

He'd admitted to having a drinking problem, and no one was ever going to give him credit for having transcended it. And if no one was ever willing to see or treat him any differently, then that meant Nils had changed for nothing.

Nils trudged back toward his office. He needed to call Crissy and make sure she'd gotten the cake. He could do it from upstairs, assuming Angie didn't have yet another unannounced surprise waiting in ambush.

He pictured her looking up at him from her desk as he passed, with those frightened little eyes, wondering if he would yell at her. He should, she'd screwed him so many times today.

No, that was the wrong thing to think about, so he shifted mental gears and returned to thoughts of Crissy and the cake, then Crissy and margaritas, all over her tits, and what the hell was wrong with him?

He'd thought he was past all that. Past the point where he was in danger of proving his father, and Paloma, and everyone else who'd never believed in him right.

But what if he wasn't?

Chapter Twelve

ROCK BOTTOM

YOU'VE GOTTA BE KIDDING me.

Nils had no idea how he should feel because every emotion seemed wrong. Or petulant. Out of alignment, perhaps. Whatever it was, Nils felt like he was running a half-mile behind all the problems in his life, and he just couldn't catch up, no matter what.

He'd only been at his desk for a few seconds, not even long enough to pull the phone from his pocket when it started to ring.

Loma flashed for the third time, and he finally answered.

"Hey, sweetheart, what's up?"

"Good afternoon, Nils. I was just calling to check in with you."

Translation, *I called to make sure you got the cake since we both knew you'd fuck it up somehow.*

"You can stop worrying. I got the cake."

"Oh, that's great," Paloma said, sounding annoyingly surprised like maybe she'd been looking forward to chewing him out for failing to remember. "Did you make sure they left a spot for the Batman action figure and—"

Shit. If Mario and his stoned friend had forgotten, she'd know he was lying about checking.

He gambled that the cake had been decorated before weed entered the picture because how would the bakery stay open if they were constantly getting orders wrong?

"Of course."

"Great. Thanks. But I actually wasn't calling about the cake."

But he'd opened his dumb mouth and brought it up anyway. "What, then?"

"I got a ping from KredIt. Someone applied for a mortgage under my name. I've already reported it as identity theft, but you might want to watch out in case someone gets your info, too."

"What happens when you report it as identity theft?"

"Seeing as this already cost me forty-five minutes I didn't have, I failed to ask about their plans for a sting operation."

"They didn't say anything?"

"Only that the matter was under investigation."

His instinct said to admit what he'd done. Better now than later. It would be one thing if he could guarantee that Paloma would never find out, but if the matter was being investigated, she probably would.

A confession in the present might save him from a much bigger fight in the future.

"They don't need to investigate."

"And why not?" Paloma asked, sounding suspicious.

"Because it was me. I—"

"*You?* Why would you apply for a loan in my name?"

"It wasn't in *your name*, it was in both our names. I was

hoping that maybe we could buy the house from my father."

Icy silence frosted his heart. It felt like a half minute before Nils dared to say, "Paloma?"

She said, "I'm here," then nothing else.

Nils wanted to defend himself, but he had been with Paloma long enough to know that even a single wrong word out of his mouth right now would only make everything worse. If he kept quiet, she'd eventually tell him what he could say to make everything right.

He was dying to hang up, confirm that Crissy had the cake, and move on to the part of this day that didn't feel like it might destroy him.

"I was only trying to help."

"I know exactly what you were trying to do," Paloma shot back before thoroughly losing her shit. "You're doing the same thing you've done since the day we met: putting your needs in front of mine and—"

"I'm not putting my needs in front of yours, I'm putting our needs as a family—"

"We're barely a family right now, Nils! Instead of skipping ahead to the finish line, why don't you focus on doing the work?"

"I have been doing the work, Paloma! I've been sober for a year."

"Sobriety has nothing to do with this, Nils. This is about you thinking you have the right to make big life decisions without asking me."

"I wasn't making any 'big life decisions,' I was researching our options."

"You applied for a loan in my name."

"Not really," Nils tried to explain. "I was just using your income and—"

"Social security number?"

This was just like her, always making a big deal out of nothing. Aside from a tiny ping on her credit record, nothing had changed. Her life was exactly the same as it had been before he'd filled out that application, except now she knew her husband loved her enough to want to stay with her forever.

There were a lot of women who'd think that was romantic, not selfish.

Like Crissy, not that she was the best example.

He didn't want Paloma to be like Crissy. But he did want her to appreciate him like Crissy did.

Her lack of appreciation was really starting to piss him off, but Nils couldn't let her know that now, not if he was expecting to reach the end of his personal rainbow.

"You haven't changed at all." She sounded furious. "I'm filing for divorce."

"Whoa. Wait. What?" Nils felt slapped. "Where is this coming from?"

"What do you mean, *where is this coming from?* I told you even before you went to rehab."

"But I'm sober now!"

"Congratulations, Nils. You fixed one problem. How are you planning on fixing the rest of them?"

"What's that supposed to mean?"

"You're unbelievable."

"At least I answer your questions. What problems are you talking about? You asked me to stop drinking, so I stopped drinking. You wanted me to start going to meetings, so I did that, too. Same as I made my home on the couch for the last year and haven't asked you for a thing. What is it you want from me, exactly?"

"I don't know, Nils, how about for you to start acknowledging all the damage you've done?"

"Whatever I did, I'm sorry."

"That's not an apology." But rather than explain, like he'd asked her to, Paloma said, "I'm through making excuses for you."

"I'm not asking you to make any excuses for me! I just want to know—"

"What you *just want* is for all of your problems to go away without you having to do the hard work of actually fixing things. That requires a lot more than meetings and sobriety."

"*I'm sorry.* I was sincerely trying to do something for our family and—"

"You always have a reason, but that doesn't make it okay. It starts with some little whatever that's easy to brush off, like using my social security number without asking me. I say *That's just Nils being Nils*, and before I know it, I'm opening the door to your bullshit."

"I'm not—"

"This isn't just about us. I need to protect our son."

"Are you kidding me?" It took everything inside him to keep *fucking* out of that sentence. Nils felt like he needed to punch a window. "I would never do anything to hurt Tyson."

"You mean *again.*"

"That was a year ago, Paloma. And I've been sober ever since. Are you really going to throw that in my face right now?"

"When should I throw it in your face?" Not that she wanted an answer. "You need to leave. Tonight. After the party."

"You can't kick me out on our son's birthday."

"I'm sorry for not kicking you out sooner."

"I haven't done anything wrong."

"Right, it's always somebody else's fault."

"That's not what I'm saying." Nils took a breath, afraid

of losing his footing even more than he already had. "I know what I did was wrong, and I've spent this last year making amends. To both of you."

"Is that what you call it?"

"Why do you say stuff like that?" Nils asked, still thinking about cough syrup and margaritas, or maybe shots of Everclear, anything to smother the outrage eating its way through him, like dusk chewing light from the day. "I have been making amends."

"No, Nils. You've been sober and going to meetings. But for the most part, you're still the same moody asshole you've been for the last few years."

"Don't call me an asshole."

"Then don't be one," she said.

"What do you want from me, yet another apology?"

"An honest first apology will do."

"I've done nothing but apologize."

She laughed. "Okay."

"Don't *okay* me."

A beat where Nils was sure he'd hear another *okay,* but then Paloma said, "*Sorry* isn't just a word, it's about acknowledgment. You can't just apologize without under-standing what you're apologizing for."

"I know what I'm apologizing for."

"Do you?" Paloma challenged him.

"I fucked up. Drank too much for too long, then bottomed out at Tyson's party."

"Be specific, Nils. How did you 'bottom out' at Tyson's party?"

"I'm sorry, okay?"

"Were you bottoming out when you showed up shirtless and covered in vomit after the cake and ice cream were gone and the presents were opened? Or was it when you took a piss in the punchbowl while laughing hysterically and yelling, 'fill 'er up!'? Was it when you picked up his tee-ball bat and asked if it was a 'dildo for worn-out porn stars' in front of Gabrielle's mother? Maybe it was when you told our son not to 'cry like a whiny little cunt' after you ruined his birthday?"

Shame nearly smothered him as he listened to her rant. He'd told his story hundreds of times in the last year, but he'd never included any of those details — because he didn't remember them.

He remembered stumbling out of the taxi Ray had called for him.

He remembered waking up in the backyard, filthy with piss and vomit, and dragging himself to the back door, only to find himself locked out.

And he remembered the fight that had driven him to go to his father for help.

But he knew what she said was true. Even if he didn't remember, his body did, a feeling of certainty deep in his bones that yes, he'd done all that.

"You never ..." He struggled to force the words past what felt like a fist around his throat. "You never told me any of that."

"For God's sake, Nils, you were there."

What could he say?

Because the person who'd done those things was him.

And how did he plug them into the humble but wise, now-I-know-better narrative of redemption he'd been repeating for the past year?

He had to say something. Had to make her understand. "You know what it was like for me growing up. My father—"

"Are you going to blame your father for everything that's wrong with you forever? Or at some point, are you going to grow the fuck up and take responsibility for your actions?"

She hung up before Nils could answer. He stared at his phone, wishing he'd let the call go to voicemail. She'd have been annoyed until he showed up at the party with the cake, but she'd have forgiven him. And he wouldn't have had to hear what he'd done at his worst.

How was he going to win her back when she remembered him like that?

The emerald pendant might not be enough of an apology.

Maybe he shouldn't try. Maybe he should focus instead on helping her see him through their son's eyes. Tyson had forgiven his father for the worst of his sins because, unlike Ed, Nils hadn't waited until his kid was all grown before changing his behavior.

Tyson was the key to winning Paloma's forgiveness.

Now Nils just had to make sure his son had a perfect birthday party.

Chapter Thirteen

ROBOTRIPPING

Nils peeked out into the reception area.

Angie wasn't at her desk, but the bottle of cough syrup was. He could see it from here.

He went back to pacing his office, grinding his heels into the carpet with his fury.

This wasn't how Day 365 was supposed to go. For the last 364 days, he'd been fueled by a singular thought: *If I can stay sober for a year, then everything can return to normal.*

More than that, Nils expected everything to be *better*.

What good were all the profound sayings and big breakthroughs in meetings if they didn't translate into his everyday life?

He'd done what he was supposed to, but no one seemed to recognize that.

The last year had proven that he could say *no* when he wanted to. It had also taught him that he didn't need alcohol and that with his shit together, he probably wouldn't ever crave it again, except for a small sip here or there. A craving he'd easily overcome when he weighed it against the love of his wife and son.

Except that Paloma wanted a divorce and maybe to keep him from seeing Tyson.

He walked to the window and stared outside. Cars and buildings and people. A world indifferent to his suffering. No, he wasn't about to boil over in rage. This was all a part of the process; that's what they said in AA. And who cared that the group he founded had fallen apart today just because Ike wouldn't listen to him and everyone left without listening anyway. Not that Nils cared, because fuck them for not appreciating everything he'd done for them.

He turned away from the window. Everything outside it was bad for him.

Nils needed the people in his life to trust him, but they refused to see him for anything other than someone he used to be. He should be aging out of this bullshit, not seeing fresh heaps of it piled onto his front porch.

He thought again about the cough syrup on Angie's desk.

What if he took one dose? Just enough to dull the edge and help him make it through this very difficult day. No one would know, and he could pretend he was coming down with a cold.

Even an imbecile could recognize the irony of his dilemma, but leaning into one vice might eliminate the odds of getting destroyed by a worse one. Like when he'd stopped at Sloppy's for a True American instead of getting his lips around a matching set of margaritas.

Nils really needed to stop thinking about that shit. Now he was licking imaginary salt from his lips.

He was hurting. People treated exterior wounds with rubbing alcohol, but Nils was injured inside. Why shouldn't he get his medicine? Angie was taking hers.

He opened his office door and peeked out into the reception area again. He could barely believe that she still wasn't back, but also whatever. Not like Nils had done any work today. Unless eroding his career counted for something. He would make the leader board for that.

He imagined taking a swig of sickly sweet syrup. Its hazy warmth. The gentle blur he both needed and deserved.

But would he be able to look himself in the mirror if he stooped so low? He'd met a woman in rehab who'd talked about robotripping. How good it had felt at first. She'd said the right dosage was ecstasy, especially if you knew how to relax and ride it through the muscle twitches, the dizziness, the hallucinations. But too much led to paranoia. Or violent behaviors, from suicide to assault.

Nils had never seen scars like hers before.

So he'd stayed away from that shit, even during the first few weeks after rehab, when he'd most wanted a drink. It made him feel superior that he'd never hit the syrup.

He could still feel superior if he took a normal dose.

The normal dose for when people got sick.

Because he didn't need to feel stoned, he just needed to feel normal.

What if somebody saw him? Anyone could walk right by at any second.

He hurried to Angie's desk and palmed the bottle as best he could, obscuring it as he slipped back into his office.

Breathing heavier than he should be, he turned the bottle in his hand and studied the label.

He locked the door behind him, then read the label again, not that he needed to. It was an excuse to keep himself from removing the lid. Lifting the bottle to his lips. Swallowing something he promised himself and those who loved him that he never would again.

He hesitated, his hand about to turn the lid. Was he really going to do this?

He unscrewed the lid and took a whiff. The medicine hit his nostrils like a bat against a ball. Like Sloppy's, it was awful yet delicious. In this case, the nasty came from its sickly sweet cherry scent, blended with the enticing fumes of alcohol that made his mouth water. He could hear the sirens singing like always, but this time Nils wondered if he should really be ignoring them.

No one would know, and he would never have to tell a soul.

One swig, then he could put the bottle back. His secret, the perfect crime.

There would be no evidence or puzzle to solve. Just a single swallow, he could start forgetting a second after it hit him. Compared to all the drinking he'd done in his life, this was a drop in the bucket. Almost literally. It was medicine, like alcohol on a wound. He really did believe that, and it wasn't his fault if others couldn't see or accept such an obvious truth.

Nils had already made it a year, what did one swallow of cough medicine matter?

Maybe no one would find out.

But he would know.

And if he collapsed only inches from the finish line, how could Nils really believe that he'd see things through to the end again?

And if he couldn't believe it, how could he ask Paloma and Tyson to believe it?

Today was all or nothing.

Nils started, surprised by the jiggling doorknob.

It jiggled again, immediately followed by a hard knock from the other side.

Nils screwed on the cap, dropped the bottle into his desk drawer, then hurried to open his office door.

Janice.

Glaring at Nils with angry eyes.

He wanted to blurt, *What did I do?*

Instead, he said, "Janice, what's up?"

"Is there a reason your office is locked?"

"No, of course not." The lightest of laughs. "I didn't even realize it was until you tried the handle. Sorry about that."

"Should I keep standing out here, or shall we step into your office?"

Nils swallowed and stepped back from the door, parting it enough for Janice to fully enter.

She sat in front of his desk, waited for Nils to take his own seat before saying, "I just got a call from a group of angry employees. Would you like to guess what they wanted?"

The workers' comp forms.

Would it be better to apologize and beg for mercy, say he'd been swamped with other things and was trying to catch up? Or should he claim that he'd thought the deadline was next week?

Somehow he didn't think either would be enough to excuse his second huge mistake in one day.

Apparently, Janice was tired of waiting for an answer. "Thanks to your negligence, we're now the defendant in a lawsuit."

Nils wheezed like he'd been punched in the gut. "If we file the forms tonight—"

"They're not just suing for expenses. They want compensation for pain and suffering. Anxiety and depression and medical complications they claim developed while we were stalling on approving treatment."

"The deadline—"

"No longer matters." Her expression was quintessential *I'm not angry, I'm just disappointed.* "I was serious when I said I didn't want Louis showing up in my office again."

"The forms were complicated. I've been trying to reach someone in the federal Office of Workers' Compensation Programs to get some of my questions answered."

"To be clear," Janice said, leaning slightly forward. "You didn't do your job because it was too difficult to do?"

"No, that's not what I'm saying." But what could he say to make this right? He fell back to begging because when life was unfair, that was the only thing that had ever worked. "Janice, please. I've been sober for a year. I'm putting my life back together."

"Are you going to make me say it, Nils?"

"You can't do this," he pleaded. "I was a little slow on a few forms, and I haven't even missed the deadline, not until midnight tonight. I can't be fired for that!"

"You can be fired for a pattern of incompetence that extends beyond this incident, including but not limited to leaving us open to a wrongful termination lawsuit from Stew."

Tequila, saki, cider, beer, wine, whiskey, vodka, rum.

Motherfucking Everclear.

"You're a liability," she added. "There's a security guard just outside, waiting to walk you to your car."

"I have rights."

"You absolutely do. Feel free to speak with a lawyer about them."

Janice stood to leave.

"I've been sober!" Nils called out behind her. "I haven't backslid, not even once."

She turned around at the door. "Coming to work sober is a baseline requirement for any job."

"I have a wife to support. And a son. Tonight's his sixth birthday."

She smiled over her shoulder at him. "Go home and enjoy the party. You wanted to leave early, right? Now you can."

Chapter Fourteen

MERMAIDS AND SUPERHEROES

CRISSY'S NEIGHBORHOOD looked an awful lot like rock bottom. He'd never realized there was an area this awful in Las Orillas. Garbage everywhere. Stores with barred windows so filthy, he doubted any light could bleed through. Seedy liquor stores and sketchy bars offering a cheap, temporary reprieve from despair.

He was still dying of a very particular thirst, even worse than before. Every block made it worse, with yet another offer to share a drink with the devil.

He passed a 24-hour donut shop that looked like they might also sell crack and a boarded-up Sloppy's only recognizable by the shape of the building beneath its layered coat of graffiti.

Then a hotel that definitely charged for rooms by the hour.

Every red light made Nils feel more vulnerable than the one before it. His doors were locked, but that might not be enough. And he'd still have to park once he arrived at her apartment.

Good thing it was still early, not quite four o'clock. He

couldn't imagine getting out of his car here after dark, not even for Tyson's birthday cake.

No wonder Crissy was such a mess, living in a place like this.

This is where you were headed.

The voice in his head sounded a lot like his father's. Nils wanted to argue that no, he wasn't, but honestly, if Ed hadn't paid for him to go into rehab, Nils might've had to crash in the rathole he'd just passed.

He could've been Crissy's next-door neighbor.

The building she lived in had to be a century old, probably more, built from stained, crumbling bricks. It looked moments from surrender, ready to collapse if anyone so much as whispered the word *earthquake.*

He got out of the car, thinking about margaritas no matter how hard he tried not to. The refrain from earlier returned, this time to the tune of a song:

Tequila, saki, cider, beer, wine, whiskey, vodka, rum — motherfucking Everclear.

Up the outside stairs two at a time. Surely someone had been murdered and left on these steps before. But no way was he trusting his life to that rickety elevator.

Maybe this was a mistake, coming here for the cake instead of asking Crissy if she could please bring it to him. He wanted everything to be easy, but when was the last time anything really was?

I've always been attracted to older men.

He could hear her sultry voice in his head, feel her squeezing his hand. Nils had done the right thing — *I'm your sponsor, not your boyfriend* — but he could tell she wasn't really listening. Even though she promised to "follow whatever guidelines he laid down," his principles should have kept Nils away from her apartment. Not just avoiding wrongdoing, but the temptation to wrongdoing.

But here he was, knocking on her door, tempting fate no less than if he were holding a bottle.

Crissy opened it and proved that his paranoia was more than appropriate.

She might as well have been naked, though seeing the full monty wouldn't be nearly as sexy as the way she looked now, barely covered in a lacy burgundy teddy that pushed her breasts up into a proud display and was so sheer in the crotch that Nils could see that she waxed.

He closed his mouth after realizing it was hanging open.

Crissy giggled and opened her door all the way. "Are you coming in or what?"

"I don't think I should." He couldn't help but rake her with his eyes. "I just came for the cake."

"I know why you came here, silly." She took his hand, pulled him inside, then closed the door behind her.

Nils had already gone too far.

He couldn't feign ignorance; he knew what was happening here.

And if he didn't get the fuck out of here now, he would regret it for the rest of his life.

But he had to bring the cake with him. Everything hinged on him making Tyson happy tonight.

"So, where is it?" His voice cracked with nerves. Then, as if she didn't know, he added, "The cake, I mean."

Crissy giggled again, clearly enjoying his discomfort. "In the refrigerator. Where else would I keep it?"

He glanced past Crissy, over her shoulder, and into the miniature kitchen. He saw an ancient fridge about the size of a nightstand that couldn't possibly be big enough to hold a full sheet cake.

Nils started toward the kitchen, but Crissy blocked his way.

"I really need to get home." He tried to ignore the burgundy teddy wrapping her lithe body. "Can I please just get the cake?"

Her arms were suddenly around his neck, and she was rubbing herself against him, her body radiating enough heat through his clothing to nearly melt his resolve.

"You and me are meant to be," she whispered.

"No." Nils slipped away from her. "Please, Crissy. The cake."

"I don't think that's why you came here."

"It is," Nils insisted, shaking his head emphatically.

"I don't believe you." She reached down to caress his cock, trying to use biology to override his humanity.

He pulled away from her again, taking a step back. "This was a mistake."

"I can tell that you want me, Nils. So here I am, do whatever you want."

I don't want you, he tried to say, but his lips wouldn't form the words. Probably because they were being controlled by the part of him that did want her.

Even though it would ruin everything.

"You saved me from myself, and now I want to save you."

His entire body begged him to say *yes,* wanting Crissy even more than it wanted a drink. If he saw a bottle of tequila on the coffee table right now, he wouldn't care.

Every second he stood there gaping at her only made it harder — literally. Crissy returned her hand to his cock and began to rub it again.

Again he pulled away.

But not too far. They were still only inches away from each other. Nils had been essentially celibate for more than a year. Paloma had started giving him an icy shoulder months before he bottomed out. He'd logged a lot of hours on FuckIt, but he'd never cheated on her.

Okay, he'd *thought about it*, but they were fantasies without intention to act, inspired by all those unrealistic scenes where the women existed only to satisfy the men. Stranded on the roadside, waiting for a pizza, or perhaps desperate to please her boss, none of it was realistic. Women didn't really answer the door in lingerie, willing and waiting and wanting to fuck.

Except that was exactly what was happening to Nils right now.

He was still arguing with himself when her lips were suddenly on his, arms around him, her soft body pressed against his hardness. He kissed her back, almost without meaning to — it had been so very, very long.

Crissy took her cue, jumping up and wrapping her legs around his waist. Time and space both made less sense than they had only seconds before.

Still kissing her, he staggered toward the kitchen, but for the first time since entering Crissy's apartment, Tyson's cake was the last thing on his mind.

He lifted Crissy onto the counter, so he could kneel and bury his face in between her legs. But Crissy's knee knocked into a stack of papers, sending the first few sheets drifting like snowfall to the floor. That ruined everything or maybe saved it.

One of the papers landed face up, a flyer with some sort of cartoon superhero caricatured at the top.

It was exactly the kind of thing Tyson would've drawn.

Nils wasn't sure if he would be taking advantage of her or she would be taking advantage of him, but either way would spell the end of everything he'd been working to rebuild. Paloma would never forgive him, and he would lose Tyson for good, which meant he was choosing to abandon his son.

Same as his own father had abandoned him.

"This isn't happening." His breath was short, but still, Nils meant what he said as he took a step back.

Crissy laughed as she lowered her panties.

"I mean it."

"Me too," she said, turning around and planting her palms on the counter, ass thrusting back toward him.

"You know what today means to me, Crissy. I just came for Tyson's cake. Please don't fuck this up for me."

She shook her ass. "If you fuck this up for me, I promise not to fuck anything up for you." Another laugh, though now it sounded dangerous.

Nils started toward the kitchen, but Crissy called out from behind him.

"I need you to fuck me, Nils!"

He opened the fridge and saw the cake box, crammed in like a king-sized pillow stuffed into a queen-sized case. He answered without looking back. "I'm your sponsor, not your boyfriend."

Crissy hopped down from the counter and grabbed his arm so hard, he spun half around.

"You know what I'm going through because you're going through the same thing. No one has to know. Please, I'm desperate for a drink. You're the only thing that can keep me sober."

Nils shook his head. "You're the only one who can do that."

She crossed her arms and pouted, bottom lip fully out. Great, now he was watching a goddamned cartoon character.

"If you leave without taking care of me, then I won't be able to resist the urges, Nils. It'll be on you if I fall off the wagon. *When* I fall off, I mean. Are you really ready to accept that responsibility?" She traced her nipples with a lazy finger, from one to the other, both of them poking against the sheer burgundy fabric as if trying to pierce it. "Or we could just do the thing you know we both want to do."

The craving was powerful, his urge to bend her over just like she wanted and furiously fuck himself into a finish. But he could already feel the regret, churning like he'd just gorged himself on another True American from Sloppy's. He'd done everything wrong, and he couldn't afford to keep making the same mistake.

Jakob had been right. Nils should never have agreed to be her sponsor. He'd done it to stroke his own ego. Pretending not to see the game she was playing or telling himself it didn't matter, that he had everything under control.

But he didn't, and now Nils was staring at the proof.

"I'm sorry, Crissy. I've let you down. I should never have agreed to be your sponsor. You need to find someone else to help you."

Nils didn't wait for a response. He turned back to the fridge and began to ease the big pink box out. It would have been better if she'd left the cake on the counter. Now the box was scrunched, both sides squeezing into the center. Same for the lid. He hoped that the frosting decorations weren't too smeared.

Box in hand, he turned around, rearing back as Crissy waved two fingers under his nose. She must have slipped them inside her because they were sticky and reeking of her.

"Last chance," Crissy said in what sounded like a warning.

"I'm sorry." Nils stepped around her, out of the kitchen on his way to the door.

"I'll tell the AA group that you took advantage of me."

He turned back, still holding the crumpled box. "If I go, you'll accuse me of doing the thing I'm refusing to do? And if I stay, I'll be doing—"

"What you want to do. What you've always—"

"No, Crissy."

"I'll tell Paloma that you came over here on your son's birthday and fucked me." Then, as if that wasn't enough, she added, "And I'll tell her you came on my face."

Nils looked at Crissy, hating himself for wanting to do exactly that. "As long as it's a lie, I can fix whatever problem you try to cause."

"When are you going to admit that your marriage is over? Paloma's your past, but I can be your—"

"If you go *anywhere* near my family, I'll get a restraining order." He'd practically growled it with a ferocity that he hadn't felt in a long time. Crissy's eyes widened in shock. "And if you feel like lying to the group, well, all I can do then is tell my side of the story and count on the fact that most everyone in the room has met their share of liars."

He reached out to open the door, but she grabbed his arm again. He yanked himself away and nearly dropped the precious cake.

"Let me go," Nils snarled as he adjusted his grip. He'd inadvertently bent the box — how much damage had he done?

He lifted the lid to take a peek.

"You've gotta be fucking kidding me." He turned back to face her. "Did you even look inside the box?"

"There's not a cake in there?"

He lifted the lid all the way so she could see inside. "Does that look right to you?"

The box was beat in on both sides, but the cake itself was fine. Beautiful, in fact. It would have made some little girl very happy.

Crissy glanced at it for barely a second, then shrugged. "How am I supposed to know if it looks right?"

"It has mermaids on it!"

"So?" She shrugged again.

"*So*, it's obviously for a girl. I don't have a daughter."

"Fuck you for not appreciating that I dropped everything to take care of this for you."

"Right. So you could ambush me here and—"

"Offer myself to you? Your kid has a fucking cake, so what's your problem?"

"IT HAS A MERMAID ON IT!"

"Boys can't like mermaids?"

"Goddammit, Crissy." Nils really wanted to hurl that pink box against the hallway wall, already stained with food and what looked like caked blood. "The bakery's closed. What the fuck am I supposed to do with this?"

"I can't believe you're being like this. I'm sorry there's a mermaid on your stupid cake, but I still don't know how I was supposed to guess that your son hated the ocean and everything in it."

"It's a superhero birthday party, but even if you didn't know that, this clearly isn't a cake for a boy."

"Again, Nils, how am I supposed to know that?" Hand on her hip, like she wasn't wrong to the last drop.

"Well, maybe the name *Kristina* written in pink icing should have been your first clue. Kristina, not Tyson."

"I took the cake that they gave me, Nils. The cake *you* asked me to please drop everything and go get. Except I don't think you ever said *please*. It was more like, *I need a favor.* Or … let me think … it was more like …" Crissy made an exaggerated face and put a finger to her chin. "That's right, you said, *You're a lifesaver. Really. Thanks a million.* Is this your idea of gratitude, Nils?"

Mad as he was, there was no point in arguing with her. This was no one's fault but his own. He'd delayed by stopping at the bank to apply for a mortgage. He'd let his frustration levels so high that he'd resorted to gorging himself on garbage food to keep from having a drink. He'd tailgated Crazy Gloria through that intersection, and he'd given in to her threat to charge him with a hit-and-run rather than walk a couple hundred feet to pick up the right cake.

He'd had the terrible judgment to call Crissy instead of confessing to Paloma and begging her to pick it up instead.

His cowardice had led to his bad decisions, and that was why his son was getting a mermaid cake instead of a superhero cake for his sixth birthday.

Because he'd wanted to be the superhero today.

And instead, he turned out to be the villain.

He hugged the box to his body and marched toward the stairs ignoring whatever Crissy yelled after him.

Into the elevator, half-hoping he would plunge to his death and not have to find out what Paloma was going to say when she saw this cake.

Down three grimy flights and out into a filthy lobby.

Onto the street, back in his car, and onto Wembley Street, still working not to weep.

Nils wished he could drain an entire bottle of Artemis Tull, then sleep it off for a week. He drove in a murderous mood. Every breath felt like a risk. Driving past bars, thoughts of drinking like raindrops atop the windshield in his mind. The world itself felt precarious, his life gliding along a thinning edge, and any second he might tip over, into an abyss without any bottom.

He was fucked. Paloma was going to kill him. And that wasn't even the worst part.

The thing that made Nils have to blink back tears, fiddle with the station, and change lanes unnecessarily just to keep himself from flying off the side of the road or starting to sob uncontrollably was imagining the disappointment on Tyson's face.

Nils would be the loser who ruined his son's childhood.

Same as Ed was the loser who'd ruined his.

He'd failed to break the cycle. His year of sobriety hadn't kept him from passing the trauma he'd inherited from his father on to his son. All the hard work he'd done meant nothing.

How had Nils become the very monster he'd sworn to slay?

Chapter Fifteen

THE CROOKED PIG

Nils had sat in a lot of dive bars in his time, but The Crooked Pig might have been the worst of them. Beer and liquor blended with stale sweat and dust. There might have been vomit too, but that could also be his memory, echoing all the times he'd gotten gassed enough to yak all over himself. That probably explained the smell of shit as well.

He couldn't have chosen a better place to question what the fuck he was doing with his life.

Another memory hit him. One he wished he could lose for good. Unfortunately, despite being completely knackered at the time, the only thing Nils had managed to forget about his misadventure was the name of the bar where it started.

After drinking himself into a fugue, Nils had apparently decided to leave the bar for a nap. He woke up in the middle of a forest, or at least a patch of woods on the opposite side of a big fence bordering a children's playground. He remembered feeling grateful for the early dawn that he didn't have an audience while scaling the fence.

Nils was even happier on the other side when he dropped to the ground feeling desperate to take a rather furious shit. He pulled down his pants to drop his pile on the ground but was still a bit slaughtered, which meant he was pooping everywhere—getting it all over both his ass and his pants. Spent again after battling both the fence and his bowels, Nils took another nap, waking up in the early morning light to the worst rash of his entire life. His skin felt like it was on fire for a week.

This was before Paloma. He'd regaled Ray with his story the following weekend as they began their next bender, turning it all into a big joke about how hardcore he could be.

Was Nils ready to surrender and fall back into that life?

"You still thinking?" The bartender checking in on him for the third time.

Now Nils was ready. "A double shot of Artemis Tull, please."

"We don't carry it," the bartender reported without apology. "How about some Old Crow?"

"Old Crow it is," Nils agreed, even though he'd wanted to drink something better. If he was going to relapse, he might as well celebrate.

The bartender nodded, then disappeared to make his illicit wish come true.

He promised himself that he'd have one drink. Then he'd head to Tyson's party and face the music.

And after Paloma screeched her displeasure at him, he'd buy himself a bottle of Tull and nurse it for the rest of the night while planning the next phase of his humiliation.

Finding a new job and a new place to live.

Maybe he could get a job as a bartender. He had an extensive knowledge of the product, and as long as he wasn't so drunk that his hands shook, he ought to be able to manage.

What in the fuck was he doing? Had he really just ordered Old Crow? That was the choice for college kids and addicts like him, he supposed. It tasted like a bitter winter, but at least it might make him feel like a man as he gulped it down before ordering another one.

He looked around the bar, hating himself for being there. But he deserved this place.

Every bar in the world was filled with losers like him, sharing the DNA of despair.

Even though he'd never been here before, he knew them.

The regulars, drinking themselves to death under dark clouds of depression and self-loathing.

The desperate cougars on the lookout for someone a little too young to defend himself, stalking the bar like an overheated jungle cat, damaged and scratched, with leathery skin and voices scarred by nicotine.

Most bars also hosted the Glory Days Gang, but not this one. There wasn't a single drinker sitting in The Crooked Pig who had ever been glorious or ever would be again. Here, even the *remember whens* had soured.

He didn't really belong here.

Sitting at the bar was still a choice.

Same for drinking the whiskey.

"Old Crow." The bartender identified the liquid misery as he set the drink in front of the drinker, as though he didn't trust Nils to remember his order.

He looked down at the drink, glad that the shithole didn't carry Artemis Tull. It would've been harder to refuse.

The fumes were making his mouth water, reminding Nils how easy it would be to numb his agony for an hour or so. Give him the strength to face the rest of this very important day.

How else could he live with the truth that he'd followed in his father's footsteps, the one thing Nils had sworn he'd never do?

He picked up the glass and held it in his hand, inhaling the fumes as he sloshed it under his nose. Tormenting himself with thoughts of how bad it could get if he took that first sip.

The unemployment line.

The shitty jobs he'd show up to drunk. And the humiliation of being fired again.

The fights over visitation. Because Paloma would know that he'd started drinking again, no matter how hard he tried to hide it.

Ed had more than two decades of hard drinking under his belt, but somehow he'd managed to come out of it unscathed. He was still lucky enough to have a nice house whose sale would fund his retirement in Florida, where he'd probably drink the rest of his life away at the VFW there.

Was Nils enough like his father to share that luck? Or would he end up living in a shithole like Crissy, broke and forgotten by the people he loved most?

This was all Ed's fault.

If Ed hadn't decided to sell the house, Nils wouldn't have been so off-balance that he flubbed the meeting with Stew.

He wouldn't have stopped at the bank at lunch to apply for a mortgage, so he wouldn't have had to eat at Sloppy's, and he wouldn't have been so late to pick up the cake. He wouldn't have rear-ended Gloria.

He wouldn't have pissed Paloma off by applying for a mortgage without her knowledge.

He wouldn't have gotten fired, because if Janice hadn't already been angry at him for mishandling Stew, she would've given him a second chance on the workers' comp thing.

Here he was, about to punish himself instead of punishing the person who'd destroyed his life.

He set his drink back on the counter and pushed it away from him.

But before throwing his life away, there was one more thing he had to do.

Years of resentment clotted his blood as Nils slammed his car door and stormed toward the VFW.

"Where do you think you're going?" asked the bouncer manning the front door, an oversized vet who looked like he'd lost track of his kills long ago.

"I'm here for my father."

"And who might that be?" But then the bouncer eyed him head to toe and answered the question for himself. "You're Ed's kid, yeah?"

"Is he here?"

The bouncer turned and bellowed over his shoulder. "Yo, Murray! You got a visitor."

"Can I just go in?" Nils asked.

"Did you risk your life while fighting a war in a foreign country?"

"No, but—"

"Then you can stand there and wait like a good little boy."

Nils stepped back, still stewing in anger but willing to wait for the father figure who was never much of a father.

The man who taught Nils every one of his most destructive habits.

The person in this world who had cost him his very best life.

By the time Ed appeared a minute or two later, Nils was about to boil over.

"What are you doing here?" Ed asked. Not *hey son, is something wrong?* Or *nice to see you.* Or even, *can I help you?*

"We need to talk."

"I thought you'd be on your way to Tyson's party."

"I knew you wouldn't be, *Grandpa.*"

"I'm taking the boy home to watch a movie afterward to give Paloma some time to herself. She deserves it."

"Don't tell me what my wife deserves."

"You need me to take care of this?" the bouncer asked Ed.

"Thanks, Wallace, but I've got it." Then to Nils. "This isn't the time."

"I'm not leaving until we have a conversation!"

"You sure—"

"I've got it, Wallace," Ed said, cutting the bouncer off. "Nils and I are going to take a walk."

So my son doesn't embarrass me in front of my drinking buddies, Nils translated.

Wallace nodded, eyeing him with suspicion as if Nils posed a genuine threat. "You let me know if you need anything."

Nils was already headed out to the parking lot, stopping near an old brown Plymouth with what looked like a brand new bumper sticker that read, *If you love your freedom, thank a vet!*

Ed, who'd followed, sighed louder and more dramatically than he needed to, obnoxious but clearly intended to let Nils feel the weight of his inconvenience.

He'd been planning this confrontation his entire life. Now that he was here, he didn't know where to start.

Ed started in the usual place. "What do you want from me, Nils?"

"A fucking apology would be nice."

"I'm sorry—"

"You don't even know what you're sorry for!"

"I'm sorry for selling my house, or whatever it is that you're coming over here to yell at me about."

"Are you sorry for ruining my life?"

But Ed only laughed in his face. "Are you fucking kidding me? If you want to slap the asshole who did this to you, then you should head inside." He jerked his thumb toward the VFW bar. "Mirror's in the bathroom."

"You're the reason I drink."

"You drink because you're weak."

"I drink because that's all I ever saw you do."

"Man up, Nils. And stop expecting the world to shake the piss off your dick. All I ever saw my dad do was yell at my mother and beat the shit out of your uncle Jesse. Have I ever hit you?"

"Maybe you needed to be around to do more than *not beat your son*."

"I was there plenty. You weren't even—"

"You traveled half the time, and you never wanted to be home even when you were in town. Mom was even lonelier than I was. That's why—"

"You don't know—"

"I'M TALKING!"

Again, Ed fell quiet.

Finally, this was the showdown he'd been preparing for his entire life. Nils was going to force his father to confront the truth.

He was going to finally act like the hero he'd always wanted to be for his son.

Nils continued. "Do you realize that I don't have a single memory of a time before you drank? When I think of you, I automatically picture you with a glass or a can or a bottle. What does that say about you? About me? *About us?* And why don't you even care?"

He didn't wait for an answer. He would have torn the head from Ed's shoulders if he tried to offer one.

"I probably wasn't even in kindergarten before I started looking for the signs to let me know you were drunk. Or I should say, the kind of drunk I shouldn't go anywhere near since you were always at least a little lacquered up. You got louder, more argumentative, took offense to simple questions. *Sorry* became a word you forgot how to say."

Nils paused. Would he offer an apology for that?

But Ed stayed stone-silent, staring back at his son with an expression Nils was unable to interpret.

Fine. The list of his father's sins was long enough to keep him ranting for a while.

"You never hit me, Dad. But I was always afraid that you would. Mom wouldn't even try to stop you from drinking. She just asked you to slow down. But you never did. We were prisoners of your addiction, and you didn't care how much it was hurting us. You couldn't have made it clearer — the bottle was more important than your family."

Nils hated himself for the tears that had started trickling down the sides of his nose. But he hated his father even more, for a monster who couldn't shed a tear himself.

"I always asked myself if there was more I could have done, but what?" Nils paused for a beat but then barreled ahead without waiting for an answer. "I was a just kid."

"I'm not arguing with any of that," Ed said after Nils finally paused long enough to allow his response. "But I still didn't make you drink."

"You're right, Dad. You didn't. But you set the example, and you were an epically awful father. Worse, you haven't changed because you're doing the exact same thing now by leading your grandson on."

"I'm not leading anyone on, Nils. I'm—"

"Planning to abandon him because you're a smug, self-righteous bastard who pretends he's perfect when you're the reason my life has gone off the rails so many times."

"That's not my—"

"I needed a father who cared about me. I needed a role model. It was your job to be there for me. And now you're moving to Florida and leaving me homeless? After everything I sacrificed to dry out?"

He hadn't meant to say that last part in a pleading voice, but somehow his anger had withered to grief. He'd spent his whole life with the knowledge that he wasn't worth being sober for. But now he wasn't even worth staying for?

"I paid for your rehab when—"

"If I broke Tyson's leg, then I'd sure as hell cover the cost of his cast! Paying for rehab doesn't mean dick if you can't even acknowledge that you're the main reason I needed it in the first place. You owe me, Dad. And it's time to pay up."

Nils gritted his teeth, trying to keep the unwanted tears from becoming ugly, snot-bubble sobs of heartbreak. Even his anger abandoned him when he needed it most.

Cars roared by on the highway behind them. It might have only been his imagination, but Nils could swear he felt Wallace staring from the VFW doorway.

"Well?" Nils finally said. "Don't you have anything to say for yourself?"

"Just waiting to see if you're done yelling at me."

"What, you don't think you deserve it?"

"You're absolutely right, Nils. I've said it before, and I'll say it again: I wasn't a good father, and I don't know how I can ever make that up to you."

"I—"

"It's my turn now," Ed said, his voice measured and perfectly in control. "I do understand the need to blame someone, so you are very welcome to keep on blaming me if that helps you get or keep your shit together. But for Christ's sake, Nils, *get your shit together.*"

"I do blame you, and it doesn't help at all!" Nils bellowed.

"Then why do you keep doing it?"

"Because I don't know what else to do!"

But … hadn't he said to Crissy, and to everyone else at his meetings, that doing the same thing over and over again but expecting different results was the definition of insanity?

Blaming Ed hadn't fixed anything or made him feel better. All it had done was remind him, over and over again, that he was a victim, doomed to live out the destiny that his father had chosen for him. That his father's drinking had trapped him in a life that he could only escape if he succeeded in a heroic effort that, frankly, left him exhausted at the end of every day.

Did he really believe that story?

He didn't, and not just because he had to leave out a lot of the details in order to feel good about telling it to other people.

Nils didn't believe it because he knew, deep down, he wasn't a hero.

A hero didn't get blackout drunk and show up at his son's fifth birthday party, covered in vomit and maybe worse, to piss in the punch bowl and call his son a whiny little cunt.

There was no way to include that truth in his epic story

of recovery without admitting that *he* was the whiny little cunt.

And he couldn't go back and stop himself from being that kind of father to his son.

But neither could Ed. No matter how much Nils wanted him to, he couldn't go back in time and stop himself from being a shitty father to Nils, either.

Another way that father and son were the same.

Did Ed feel the gut-wrenching guilt that Nils did every time he looked Tyson in the eyes?

Did he taste bitter hatred for his own father every time Nils accused him of not doing enough?

Did he secretly hate himself for all the missed chances and lost moments?

Nils was lucky because he had the rest of his son's life to make up for one horrible birthday and a long month of absence.

What would it be like to know that he'd failed Tyson for eighteen years? Or more?

That was Ed's hell.

But it wouldn't be his. He would find a way to fix this. He would apologize.

You can't just apologize without understanding what you're apologizing for. How many times had Paloma said that to him in the last 364 days?

Dozens. Maybe more.

He'd apologized to her hundreds of times. But Nils had been apologizing for the wrong things. Every one of his *sorrys* had been a complaint, or a demand, or an attempt to manipulate her into doing what he wanted her to do.

And when that didn't work — because Paloma understood him better than he understood himself — he fell back into bitterness that hurt him more than it hurt anyone else.

"I'm an idiot," Nils finally said.

His father sighed. "You and me both, son. But at least it's not too late for you."

Chapter Sixteen

PIRATE PIZZA

Even if Nils wasn't dying for a drink, Pirate Pizza still would have made him want to blow his brains out.

The pizza was worse than the slop they served at Sloppy's: salty, greasy, with a rubbery crust that was somehow worse than any frozen pizza he'd ever eaten.

Various colored lights on the walls and ceiling flashed at irregular intervals for no apparent reason.

The animatronics sang corny, watered-down sea shanties whose lyrics were loaded with puns and told knock-knock jokes so moronic no human being could've uttered them with a straight face.

As for the games, what six-year-old had a chance in hell of winning at skeeball? And did anyone play whack-a-mole these days?

For some reason, their logo was a giant squid with glowing red eyes. Underneath it, they should've posted a sign that said: *Abandon all hope, ye whose children have birthday parties here.*

But it was what Tyson had wanted.

The place was chaos, the kids all running around like

lunatics on crack, but he didn't see Paloma or Tyson anywhere. He felt both anxious and relieved. Anxious, because Nils really did want Tyson to know he was there for his very special day, but also relieved that he could avoid the look of disappointment when he saw the cake for at least a little longer.

He decided to order a Coke to sip while he waited. A little bit of sugar to make the medicine Paloma would undoubtedly give him go down.

Nils hugged the box containing the mermaid cake closer to his chest and approached the counter, still on the lookout for Paloma, his son, or anyone else he might recognize.

"Ahoy matey," said the eyepatch-wearing cashier, without any pirate's inflection or irony, either. Nils figured she'd suffered enough indignity, so what the hell.

"Welcome to Pirate Pizza. Would you like to order a Davy Jones Locker, now with twice the cheese?"

"*Davey Jones Locker?* Isn't that a graveyard at the bottom of the ocean for people who have been killed or drowned? What does that have to do with food?"

She shrugged but said nothing.

Nils couldn't stop his curiosity. "What's in the Locker?"

Her eyes flicked to the side as if referencing a menu. "One large pizza, with your choice of topping, and now with twice the cheese. Plus fruit cocktail."

"Fruit cocktail?" Fuck this place. "Can I just get a Coke, please?"

"Gold Doubloon or Buried Treasure?"

"What's the difference?" Nils asked.

"Buried Treasure is bigger." Now the cashier's inflection suggested that Nils was an idiot.

"I'll take the large one." He couldn't bring himself to call it *buried treasure*.

She poured the drink, set it on the counter, and charged him three dollars more than it was worth.

He said *thank you* without meaning it, then moved the cake box, so he was balancing it with one hand while he took a sip of his Coke. It didn't kill his desire to get the hell out of there, but at least it was cold and fizzy.

There were too many sounds clashing and clanging around him, and the flashing lights were already giving him a headache.

"Nils?"

He turned toward the voice and saw a woman he recognized from somewhere; he just wasn't sure where. But the only people here who would recognize him would be parents of kids who'd attended Tyson's party last year.

In other words, someone who had been around for his bottoming out.

As much as he'd worried about this day going well, it had never occurred to him to worry about that.

The wave of nausea that flooded through him made the impending headache ten times worse. Whatever she wanted to say to him, he deserved it.

He forced himself to wait as she approached.

"Maria," she said, waving a manicured hand at Nils. "I'm Javier's mom. Thank you so much for inviting us. Javi's really been looking forward to this."

Nils stopped himself from glancing around the place and from asking *why?*

"I'm so glad you guys could make it."

Maria nodded at the box. "Looks like the cake had a hard day."

"Yeah." Nils had nothing to add. Apparently, neither did Maria.

"Well," Maria said, working to sound chipper. "Thanks again for inviting us!"

"My pleasure." Then, because pirates, he added, "Batten down the hatches and shiver me timbers."

Maria turned and walked away, leaving Nils feeling bad for being an antisocial asshole and grateful that he wouldn't have to explain the simple mistake that made him look like the thoughtless father he wasn't.

But his reprieve was short-lived. Walking back toward the ball pit, he saw Paloma coming toward him, hands outstretched for the cake.

She didn't smile as she stopped in front of him, just offered a tight, slight nod. "You made it."

He wanted to snap at her. Something like, *Of course, I made it.* But that was only his weaker instincts shoving their way to the front of his psyche. She didn't deserve to hear any of the self-righteous excuses Nils normally issued when Paloma acted like he couldn't be trusted.

She took the box out of his hand, gentle yet insistent.

"Before you look in the box, there's something I need to tell you."

But Paloma was already lifting the lid to peek inside. One glance, then she was glaring at him. "Are you fucking kidding me?"

"I'm not sure that language is Pirate Pizza approved," Nils tried to joke.

But Paloma wasn't in the mood. "You had *one* thing to do."

"And I did it," he said, keeping his voice light, which sometimes helped. "We have a cake, don't we?"

"It has a mermaid on it!" That time Paloma was loud enough to invite a couple of glances, including one from Maria, who was two tables over and pretending not to look.

"Boys can like mermaids," he argued.

"Our son is having a superhero party. And even if this cake wasn't pink with mermaids and seashells, it doesn't even have his name."

"It's not like he can read," Nils said, instead of *sorry*.

"He knows his letters and that his name doesn't start with a K!"

Nils took a breath and said the hard thing. "I'm sorry. There was a mix-up at the bakery."

"Why did you lie to me?"

"I didn't—"

"I asked you, Nils. I asked if the cake was right, and you lied to me about it."

"I didn't know."

"That's exactly what I'm talking about! How could you not know? You're the one who picked it up. You're the only one who *could* know!"

Paloma kept getting louder. More people were watching. "Can we talk about this l—"

Something slammed into his knees before he could finish.

Tyson, hugging his leg like a favorite stuffed animal.

Nils scooped the boy up and plastered kisses on his head.

"I've been waiting and waiting and waiting for you to come," Tyson said.

"And I've been waiting all day to get here."

Tyson hugged him again, harder this time. "Malory came as Superman, but she's a girl."

Nils set his son on the floor, made sticky by an army of scurvy dogs and scallywags. "That's what costumes are for. Malory can pretend to be anyone she wants to be."

Tyson crossed his arms. "Superman is a boy. She should be Supergirl."

Nils said, "Maybe Malory doesn't like Supergirl."

"Then Malory wouldn't be wrong," Paloma replied, surprising Nils with a joke and the thinnest of smiles.

Tyson tightened his crossed arms and insisted, "Girls aren't allowed to be boys."

"Why not?" Nils asked.

"Because boys aren't allowed to be girls."

Nils got to his knees and looked at his son. "Says who?"

"You, Daddy."

He blanched. "When did I say that?"

"Last Halloween, when I wanted to be Joy from *Inside Out*. You said that Joy was a girl and that boys aren't allowed to be girls."

Nils didn't remember saying that, but if Tyson had heard it, he wasn't about to gaslight his son. "I was wrong. Boys can be girls, and girls can be boys. I must've been distracted if I said something else."

"So, I can be Wonder Woman if I want?"

Nils pulled his son into a hug. "You would make an excellent Wonder Woman."

He looked up, saw Paloma smiling, and felt something like hope.

"I'm so so SO glad you came, Daddy."

"Of course, I came. I wouldn't have missed it for anything."

"Mommy said you might be too busy."

That broke his heart. Nils couldn't count the number of times he had heard that bullshit excuse from his own mother. It was exactly what she used to tell him when Ed didn't show or to prepare Nils when she was sure he wouldn't.

"I'm sorry I missed a lot of stuff this year, little dude. I'm not going to let it happen again."

That was when he noticed Tyson wasn't in costume.

"Where's your mask?"

"I was waiting for you!" He scurried off to a nearby table, returning with the masks. He held Batman out in offering to Nils.

"I think I feel more like Robin tonight." He donned the Boy Wonder mask, then helped Tyson line Batman's eyeholes up with his eyes.

He couldn't see Tyson's giant smile from behind the plastic cowl, but it was easy enough to imagine. He jumped up and down, squealing. Then he stopped, and in a serious voice, lower than Nils had ever heard him go, he growled, "I'm *Batman.*"

And he scampered off into the arcade area to join his superhero friends.

Nils watched him go, wondering how many other moments like this he'd missed.

He wouldn't miss out on anything else, not ever again.

Chapter Seventeen

ONE YEAR TONIGHT

Nils slowly approached Paloma at the cake table.

For a moment, things seemed like they might be fine, but the closer he got to her, the more that felt like wishful thinking. She was positioning a pack of DC action figures around the cake. Batman and Robin, of course, but Nils also saw Wonder Woman, Batgirl, Flash, and Aquaman. The whole Justice League, give or take. The mermaid loomed in the middle, like a goddess for the heroes to worship. Paloma had smeared the frosting, turning *Kristina* into an asymmetrical pink swirl and plopping Wonder Woman down roughly in the center.

Her movements were precise yet jerky. Paloma seemed madder now than she had when he arrived.

And it occurred to him that, as humiliated as he'd felt when Maria had approached him, Paloma's humiliation was probably ten times worse. She'd had to see those same parents every day when picking their son up from school. Every time she volunteered at an event. Whenever Tyson went on a playdate.

That was the thing he'd never apologized for. The

ongoing, everyday humiliation of having to live down something that hadn't even been her fault. Having to help Tyson understand that it wasn't his fault, either.

And maybe wondering if Nils was going to humiliate them again tomorrow.

How had he never seen that?

She finally finished the cake. It looked ridiculous but better than anything Nils would have thought to do.

She'd had a lot of practice at turning his mistakes into something that looked intentional and managing Tyson's disappointment.

Paloma positioned the final hero on the cake, adjacent to the mermaid's wide-open mouth. Due to the size difference between the mythical sea creature and the superhero standing upright beside it, the mermaid looked like it was about to eat the action figure. Aquaman did somehow seem like the most appropriate choice.

"I'm sorry," he said to her.

"It's just a cake." But Paloma didn't mean that.

"No." Nils circled the table to face her. "I mean, I'm sorry for everything I've put you through. I'm sorry for always leaving you to deal with the shit parts of parenting. I'm sorry for taking all of your support and patience for granted. I'm sorry for not constantly thanking you for how much you've done for me, ever since I've known you and especially this last year. I wouldn't have been able to stay sober if it wasn't for you."

His voice cracked at the end, and Nils had to press a hand to his heart so he could maybe calm it down, but at least it was all out of him.

Paloma blinked a few times, then stared into his eyes, seeming to study him. She looked suspicious as if expecting a trick.

"I still want a divorce."

"I understand. I won't fight you on anything. All I ask is that we share custody."

Silence, heavy and long and inescapable, but also comforting, in a way. There was nothing left to deny. Nothing to fight about.

"What were you thinking?" Paloma finally asked.

He looked at her blankly. There were so many things she could have meant.

"Applying for a mortgage in my name," she answered the question he hadn't asked.

That I missed my family.

That I deserved to be rewarded for getting sober.

That I was afraid of losing Tyson.

"I guess I was hoping that things would go back to normal," Nils admitted. "Like they were before."

"But they were never normal." Paloma wiped the tear away the second it started to fall.

"You're absolutely right," he said.

She looked back at him in what could only be described as *wonder.* "I don't think you've ever said that to me."

He hadn't because he'd been too busy feeling wronged. "You've been right about a lot of things."

Another tear, but Paloma let this one go. "What's going on with you?"

He opened his mouth to tell her about everything — including getting fired. But the last thing in the world he wanted to do was make any part of tonight about him.

"My dad told me that you already have a place lined up for after the sale goes through."

Paloma stiffened. "He didn't tell you that he's selling it to me?"

"What? How can you—"

"I had a separate savings account I never told you about. Plus, I landed a big bonus at the end of last year. And no offense, but now that our finances are separate, it's been easy to stay on a budget."

"I'm sorry I made it so hard for you," Nils said. "I mean that."

"I can tell." Her voice was softer than it had been in so long.

Nils wondered what else she had been keeping from him, or more precisely, what else he had lost the right to know. But that was on him. The only thing that mattered was that his son had a safe place to stay.

"It's a great house to grow up in. Tyson will be really happy there."

"You can keep living in the guest house if you want. For Tyson."

Something melted inside him. Nils could feel an old need turning to vinegar and a new one assuming its place. Clean and pure and slightly sweet, like water from a snowcap.

"Thanks." He was grinning like an idiot, but he didn't care who saw. "I'd like that."

Paloma smiled back. "Congratulations, by the way."

"For what?"

"One year tonight, right?"

She'd remembered.

Which meant she cared. Maybe not in the way he'd been hoping when he'd bought the emerald necklace — which he would return tomorrow, but in a way that meant more to him than that one-year chip ever could.

"One year tonight," he agreed.

Nils couldn't start over, but he could start again.

After spending his entire adult life either getting drunk

or dying to, Nils was finally ready to start drinking from his life.

It wouldn't be easy, but it would be worth it.

What to read next

**He sacrificed his family for ambition —
but now they're all he has left.**

Action movie director, Cameron Parrish, wants to make real cinema. But hours after being greenlit to make the film of his life, he's diagnosed with terminal brain cancer. Desperate to make his final days matter, he joins a program to help him discover the meaning of his life and death.

Get The Final Frame Today

A Quick Favor...

If you enjoyed this book, please take a moment to write a short review on your favorite online bookstore so other readers can enjoy it, too.

Thanks so much!
   Harmony Reed

About the author

Harmony Reed writes revelatory stories about what it means to live, how we can become more fully human, and how we can shed the lies we've been living by and embrace our truth. Her fiction melds the large-scale with the deeply-personal, yielding insight into the human psyche and the world we all must move through. If you enjoy authors like Michael Chabon and Jodi Picoult, movies like *Big Fish* and *Little Miss Sunshine*, or shows like *Orange is the New Black* and *This is Us*, you'll love Harmony Reed.

Also by Harmony Reed

Spitting Image

Drink

La Fleur de Blanc

Confidence John

The Final Frame